A FOREVER
KIND OF GUY

A FOREVER KIND OF GUY

•

FRANCES ENGLE WILSON

AVALON BOOKS
THOMAS BOUREGY AND COMPANY, INC.
401 LAFAYETTE STREET
NEW YORK, NEW YORK 10003

PRINTED IN THE UNITED STATES OF AMERICA
ON ACID-FREE PAPER
BY HADDON CRAFTSMEN, BLOOMSBURG, PENNSYLVANIA

To Doug and Randy,
Two of the best, who walk tall and
do not fear to climb the highest hill

The whirling wind did havoc make,
Leaving sadness in its wake.
And years go by till light is cast,
To dispel shadows from the past.

Chapter One

Summertime in Claysun, Oklahoma, was the usual unending series of long, hot days, with the kind of sun-baked temperatures that accounted in part for the town being called Clay-sun. For this energetic city got its name from the fact that it was surrounded by hills of gray shale and rested on the clay banks of the Silverline River, whose gently moving water shone as lustrous as burnished pewter under the brilliant rays of the southwestern sun.

Megan Manford walked quickly down the air-conditioned corridors of the hospital, a pleased smile on her tanned face. Her features were an attractive blend of a small, slightly turned-up nose, a wide mouth, and intelligent, humorous brown eyes. She had an air of quiet competence about her, due in part to the fact that she'd just finished her first week in her new job. She was smiling because she felt confident that she'd gotten off to a good start. But then, she'd expected to, because she was well qualified, computer-wise, and therefore ready and able to assume the position of Supervisor of Medical Records at Claysun's old and prestigious St. Mark's Hospital.

As she reached the exit adjacent to the emergency room she slowed her steps, dreading the thought of stepping out into the hundred-degree July heat. Megan heaved a weary sigh, then staunchly pushed the outside door open and headed out the back of the hospital. She went down the narrow alley to get to the parking area reserved for doctors and those who worked at St. Mark's. Weaving her way through the rows of parked cars, feeling the heat rising off the black asphalt, she wished she hadn't parked clear away in the far corner of the lot. But it had seemed a good idea this morning when she arrived because it was a remote spot that was shaded by the overhanging tin roof of a nearby run-down building.

Both the heat and the silence were oppressive. Megan found the stillness unsettling, for there didn't appear to be anyone else around the lot. Of course, there wasn't likely to be this late in the day. The comings and goings here in the staff parking area occurred when the nursing shifts changed at seven, three, and eleven.

Approaching her cherry-red Ford Escort, Megan pulled her car keys from her purse and unlocked the door. As she withdrew the key from the lock, suddenly a man's sweaty hand clamped down savagely over hers.

"Nice shiny car you got here, honey. How about you and me going for a ride?"

Megan let out a startled cry and tried to jerk her hand away.

"Oh, you wanta play games, huh?" The man grabbed her viciously by both arms, a lewd grin twisting across his face.

Screaming in terror, Megan tried to wrench herself from his grasp. The man clenched the tender flesh of her upper arms, and before she knew what was happening, he slammed his body hard against her, throwing her down onto the narrow strip of pavement between the Escort and the car parked next to it.

Crying out in fear, Megan struggled to fight him off. He hit her with his fist and then slapped each side of her face. She recoiled in horror as he bent his dirty, ugly face close to hers. Fighting him with all the strength she had, she kept screaming.

"Hey, what in blazes is going on out there?" A

man's voice yelled. Then Megan heard the rapid fall of running footsteps. "Leave her alone, you animal!"

Someone had grabbed hold of her attacker and was yanking him away, freeing her. She made an effort to get up, but her chest was heaving from the pounding of her heart, and a spinning sensation in her head was making her somewhat dizzy. She took several deep breaths to steady herself as she slowly sat up. Still feeling stunned, she took in the violent conflict going on between the stranger who had mugged her and the courageous young man who had miraculously come to her rescue.

Aware now that she had to do something—go for help, get the hospital security guard—something, anything, she struggled to her feet. At that moment, in the fracas in front of her, she saw a sudden flash of metal.

She screamed out in horror at the sight of the shiny steel knife in the grime-stained hand. The mugger lunged at the younger man, viciously slashing at him. A flow of crimson blood soaked through the shoulder and left sleeve of the fellow's white knit shirt, then ran down to make grotesque red stains on his light-colored slacks.

"Now who's the animal?" the attacker snarled. Then, mouthing curses, he fled, darting behind Megan's car and disappearing around the side of the deserted, tin-roofed building at the back corner of the parking lot.

Anxiously, Megan eyed the injured man. "You stay still," she told him. "I'm going to the hospital to get help for you."

He shook his head. "I can make it all right," he insisted, beginning to walk ahead, his right hand pressed flat against his left shoulder.

"Are you sure?" Megan asked, seeing the blood oozing through his fingers where his hand couldn't stem the flow. "You're really bleeding a lot."

"It'll only take us a couple of minutes to get to the emergency room." He glanced at her, a concerned look in his vivid blue eyes. "You need attention, too, you know. That scum of a man slapped you around plenty." His voice was harsh, and the clenched thrust of his jaw mirrored both his anger and his pain as he lengthened his stride, walking faster.

Megan hurried along beside him, tight-lipped and tense with fear. A desperate panic engulfed her at the sight of the increasing bloodstains spreading over his shirt. What if that knife had hit an artery? Even a vital organ? What if he was also bleeding internally? This brave, helpful man had saved her from real harm. Was it possible that he could now die? She gasped, a dreadful apprehension sweeping through her, and even in this extreme heat she felt chilled to the bone as if overwhelmed by unbearable cold.

The second they reached the door into the emergency room, Megan called out for help. A robust orderly and a plump, maternal-looking nurse rushed toward them.

"Good grief, it's Dr. Hadley!" the nurse cried. "It looks bad." She yelled back over her shoulder. "Have them page Dr. Kane to get to the ER stat! Tell him Tucker Hadley has been hurt."

"He's been stabbed. There was a man in the parking lot. He had this awful-looking knife." Megan's excited stream of words were lost in the flurry of activity that now surrounded her. The injured doctor was whisked away, and Megan was taken into a curtained-off cubicle where an intern took her blood pressure, listened to her chest, checked the pupils of her eyes, and then proceeded to examine the bruises on her face. Before he had completed his examination a hospital security officer came in to question her about exactly what had occurred in the parking lot. She was giving the officer a description of her assailant when the kind-faced nurse she'd met earlier came in carrying a shiny metal washbasin in her hands.

"Dr. Hadley wanted you to put a cold compress on your face," she said as the uniformed guard turned away and left the two women alone. "It will help reduce the swelling and ease the pain,'' she said, handing Megan a small, thick pad that had been soaked in very cold water.

''Thank you. That does feel good,'' Megan said, holding the compress to her battered cheek. ''I'm not hurt too much, actually, thanks to your great Dr. Hadley. I'm terribly worried about him, though. He was bleeding so much. Tell me, how bad is he? D-do you think . . . I mean, he will be all right, won't he?''

''Dr. Kane was with him when I left. They were working to get his bleeding stopped.''

Megan's face clouded with uneasiness. ''He shouldn't have walked from the parking lot. I tried to stop him. I wanted to get help, but he wouldn't let me.''

The nurse bobbed her head, a knowing look on her face. ''That's just like Tucker Hadley. He's stubborn, all right. And though he doesn't always take care of himself, he always takes particular care of his patients. You've seen an example of that right here.'' She glanced down at the basin she still held in her hands, then looked at Megan and smiled. ''Instead of being concerned because his bleeding wasn't under control, he was telling me to see about getting these cold compresses for your bruised face.''

''Oh, he did much more than that.'' Megan

sighed, a glint of moisture in her concerned eyes. ''I'll be forever in his debt for what he did for me, and I haven't even thanked him.'' She flung out her hand in a gesture of simple despair. ''I'm so anxious about him. I've got to know that he's going to be all right.'' She frowned and bit the corner of her lip. ''Look, is there someplace where I can wait and maybe get a chance to see him for a minute, or at least talk to this Dr. Kane who you said was tending to him?'' she implored.

The older woman reached out and patted Megan's arm. ''You stay right here and use that compress for twenty minutes or so,'' she said, a calming note in her patient voice. ''I'll check on Dr. Hadley and ask if he might be able to see you for just a few minutes after they've closed those knife wounds of his. Shouldn't be too much longer.'' With a reassuring smile the nurse hurried off, leaving Megan alone in the curtained-off stall.

Sometime later an aide came to tell Megan that it was all right for her to speak to Dr. Hadley. ''He's in room 434,'' the aide said, pointing in the direction of the elevators.

Megan thanked her, laid the wet compress aside, and left the ER. She took the elevator to the fourth floor, then walked rapidly along the corridor until she came to the right room. The door was pushed totally open. She hesitated, reached her hand inside, and gave a couple of quick knocks. "It's Megan Manford, Dr. Hadley," she announced before she entered.

Tucker Hadley was sitting up in bed, a major part of his upper torso swathed in bandages and his left arm in a sling. She eyed him anxiously, her concerned expression further marking her battered face, which now showed discoloring bruises along her cheekbones.

"How are you doing?" she asked, walking closer to the bed.

"All right, I think."

"It's really bad, isn't it?"

Tucker made an effort to smile. "No. Not too bad."

"Are you sure?"

"Yeah. I'm sure. Most of the wounds were fairly superficial. I was lucky."

Her questioning eyes searched his haggard face. "But you were bleeding so much. I was frightened for you."

"Hey, your father was a doctor. You have to know that some blood tends to make things look worse than they actually are."

She cocked her head, looking at him curiously. "How did you know my father was a doctor?"

"Well, when they told me your name was Megan Manford, I asked if by any chance you were related to Dr. Adam Manford, who was head of pediatrics here at St. Mark's back in the eighties. They said you were his daughter.''

''Right, I am. But you don't look old enough to have been practicing medicine here that long ago,'' she said with a quizzical smile narrowing her eyes. ''So, how did you know him?''

''I didn't know him really. But I had occasion to see him from time to time, and I admired him.'' Tucker's expression brightened and some of the weariness vanished from his eyes. ''You see, I worked as an orderly here at St. Mark's during several summers while I was in college. Now a dozen or so years later I meet the good doctor's daughter.'' Tucker extended his unbandaged right hand to her. ''I could wish it had been under less painful circumstances, however.''

''Me, too!'' Megan agreed emphatically as she enclosed his hand in both of hers. ''You know, there really is no way I can ever thank you enough for what you did for me,'' she said, still holding his hand firmly pressed between hers. ''You risked your life to protect me, and I shall never stop being grateful.'' Her voice revealed the depth of her feelings and her eyes were luminous with tears. Not wanting to embarrass him with this show of emotions, she released his hand and turned quickly away. ''I promised not to stay more than three or four minutes,'' she said quickly. Then before he could say anything, she added, ''Take care—goodbye,'' then hurried out of his room.

As Megan approached the elevators, a man wearing a white doctor's coat came from the opposite corridor at the same time. ''You going up or down?'' he asked, one hand poised over the signal buttons.

''Down,'' she said, glancing at his name tag pinned to the pocket of his slightly rumpled coat. Evan Kane, M.D.—why, that was the name of Tucker Hadley's doctor. She appraised the tall, redheaded doctor with quickened interest. ''You're the doctor who treated the knife victim—''

''You're the lady in the parking—''

They both had started speaking at the same time. Evan stopped in mid-sentence, eyeing her with laughter in his tortoise-colored eyes and a broad grin on his lightly freckled face.

''Tucker Hadley is my friend and associate. The two of us are in practice together,'' he explained. ''He told me all about what happened out there and made me promise to get your injuries attended to and also find out your name and all about you. So I know you're Megan and you know I'm Evan and we both have a vested interest in Tucker. Right?''

''That's right!'' Megan raised her voice emphatically. "I've just come from seeing him. He says he's okay. Is that really true?"

"Mostly. Of course, he will need to take it easy for a day or two. But basically Tucker's strong as an ox; problem is, he's stubborn as one, too. You should have heard him bellow at me because I insisted he had to stay in the hospital overnight. He's a great doctor, but a lousy patient."

The elevator arrived and Megan stepped on, expecting Evan Kane to join her. When he didn't, she looked at him inquiringly. "I'm going up," he said. The doors slowly closed then and the elevator started down.

With all that had happened, Megan had lost track of the time. Now, even though the sun had set, the summer heat still cloaked the city. As she drove home there was hardly a breath of wind to stir the elms and maples that lined the parkway. At the sight of the iron fence covered with thick ivy that surrounded the Manford house, she felt a rush of nostalgia. How thankful she was that she hadn't let the family attorney talk her into selling this home two years ago when her parents were killed in a plane accident. She'd grown up in this comfortable stone house with its crab apple trees and even now that she lived here alone, it was still her haven and refuge.

She turned into the driveway and parked her car

near the flagstone walk that led to the front door. Probably it was because she was still in an emotional state, but she didn't get out of the car right away. Instead she leaned wearily back against the seat and covered her bruised face with her hands. A soul-deep sigh shuddered through her, slowly starting to narcotize the nerves of her body. She was home. She was safe. Whatever even more harmful experience she could have suffered, she had been spared because of a nice young doctor, who strangely enough had once known and admired her father. Somehow she wanted to think there was something significant in this fact.

Contemplating this, she closed her eyes, conjuring up Tucker Hadley in her mind. She would not call him handsome, though his nice, average features did add up to something appealing that she would not easily forget. She recalled that when she was walking beside him in the parking lot that he was slightly taller than medium height, and his body was sturdy and well muscled. His sun-streaked blond hair grew thick above his forehead, and there was a dark flash in his eyes that could surprise with its intensity. Yes, she thought, the feature that could be called handsome about him was his eyes. And their beauty lay in their expression as well as their color, which Megan remembered as being deep marine blue.

How beholden she felt to this Tucker Hadley. Letting her hands fall away from her face, Megan opened her eyes in a look of wonderment, sensing for the first time that the debt she owed him now formed a unique bond between them.

Chapter Two

Word of the knifing incident filtered into all areas of the hospital, causing a stir of excitement and considerable apprehension. By the beginning of the following week several precautionary measures had been taken which included routine patrols of both the staff parking area and the visitors' larger parking lot.

Although Megan didn't go into St. Mark's over the weekend, she did call and inquire about Tucker on Saturday. She was encouraged to learn that he'd been released that morning. So obviously after one night in the hospital he was doing fine, or like Evan Kane had stated, he was stubbornly deter-

15

mined to end his patient status and do his recuperating at home.

As for Megan, by Monday the swelling was almost gone from her face; however, she still had bruise marks across her cheekbones, and some slight discoloration along the left side of her jaw. She experimented with a bit of liquid makeup which camouflaged most of it. Then when she added a tawny blush and light coral lipstick, she decided she looked almost normal. She had gotten up early to have time to shampoo her shoulder-length auburn hair. Now she brushed it back and tied it with a chiffon scarf the same lime green color as the trim on her white linen dress.

The residential area where Megan lived was on the south side of Claysun. In the early-morning rush-hour traffic it would take her sometimes twenty-five minutes to get to the hospital. However, since she didn't have to be in the records office until nine o'clock, she usually waited until the traffic thinned out after eight-thirty, for then she could drive in to St. Mark's in a record fifteen minutes. This Monday as she headed out, morning sunlight was already flooding Willow Wood Park and the buildings around it. A jogger, a middle-aged man wearing gray shorts and sweatshirt, dirty running shoes, and a headband, chugged across the intersection to Megan's left and trotted into the park. Pigeons gawked along the sidewalks and dust blew skittishly across the pavement of the street, while rising heat made shimmery waves off parked cars at the curb. Two miles further on, an electronic sign on the Claysun National Bank building said it was 8:48, and the temperature was already 88 degrees. Megan shook her head and sighed. The sky was cloudless, so the sun would be unmerciful. She'd bet Claysun would top the hundred mark by lunch time.

Megan entered at the front of the hospital this morning. She walked quickly by the information desk and the admitting office, then down a buff-colored corridor that smelled faintly of disinfectant. The heels of her white pumps made a sound like clicking castanets on the terrazzo floor.

"Hey, Megan, wait a second."

She stopped and turned around to see Tucker walking toward her. "Hi," she called, raising her hand in a surprised but pleased salute.

"I had two patients I needed to check on this morning before I went over to my office. I was hoping I might get lucky and run into you," he said as he caught up with her.

She smiled up at him. "I'm so glad you're feeling up to seeing patients. That's great. You're looking good, too."

"You're the one who's looking good," Tucker

said, giving her a head-to-toe appraisal, undis-
guised interest sparking his smiling eyes. He
leaned closer to scrutinize her face. "Swelling is
gone. Bruising is minimal. I'd say there's been no
permanent damage to this pretty face of yours."

"Is that your professional opinion, Doctor?"
she asked, laughing.

He grinned. "Both professional and personal."

"Then I don't need the service of a plastic sur-
geon."

"No, but I can recommend a good internist for
future maladies."

"I'd say you already have," she said, taking a
frank and admiring look at him.

They exchanged a subtle look of amusement.
Then Tucker gave a quick glance at his wristwatch. "I've got patients waiting at the office. I'd
better run." He turned away. "See you around,"
he said as he headed off.

Megan's mood was now bright. She felt good
about this brief encounter with Tucker. She hadn't
expected to see him at the hospital today. The fact
that he was able to carry on his normal routine this
soon surprised her. Either he was recuperating
amazingly well, or he had put on a stalwart front
for her benefit. Probably it was a little of both, she
thought.

She quickened her steps, for she realized it was

after nine and she should be in the office. There was a lilt now in her walk as she hurried along. Satisfaction pursed her mouth as she recalled Tucker's complimentary words on her appearance. Thank goodness she'd taken extra pains with her makeup. And tying the green scarf around her hair had been an inspired touch, she thought with smug delight. Her mother had told her many times that green was the ideal accent color for her hair and eyes. Mothers were always right about things like that. A ripple of laughter played across her lips at the foolishness of her thoughts.

There had been merely a brief account in the newspaper concerning the incident at St. Mark's. It stated that two people had sustained injuries in the attack, but did not list the names. Megan was thankful for this, as the fewer people who knew about it, the sooner the whole thing could be over and forgotten.

It was generally known around the hospital, however, that she and Tucker were the parties involved. So it wasn't surprising that a few of the older staff members who'd worked with her father stopped by her office during the morning to inquire about her.

Shortly before noon, Dr. Bruce Samuels came in to see her. The obstetrician had a bristle of iron-gray hair and the type of face sometimes described as "winged." The corners of his mouth made two deep depressions such as a painter would render with a crisp upward stroke of the brush. His nostrils, too, slanted up, and so did the outside corners of his graying eyebrows.

"Just heard about the fracas you were in Friday afternoon. Wanted to see for myself that you were all right," he said, concern softening his normally gruff voice.

"I'm fine, thanks to Tucker Hadley. He suffered the brunt of it."

"Yeah, I heard that." He was studying her face, and now a thoughtful expression tightened his lips. "You know, Megan, your father would be so pleased that you finally came back to Claysun to work here at St. Mark's. You stayed away a long time. How many years has it been, anyway?"

"Well, counting college and all, I guess it's been about seven and a half years," she said, fingering a paper clip lying on her desk. "You see, while I was getting a degree in business geared toward hospital management, I worked part-time at Southwestern University Hospital. When I finished school I went to work full-time there."

"I remember now," he said, bobbing his head and making a slight clicking noise with his teeth.

''At your parents' funeral somebody mentioned that you were in management training at a small hospital in a college town.''

She smiled and nodded back at him. ''Right. And I stayed there until I got an opportunity to interview here at St. Mark's. I grabbed at that chance, of course. Not only because St. Mark's is a much larger hospital, but it meant I'd be back on home turf.'' Her smile broadened. ''How lucky can a gal get?'' she asked gleefully.

Dr. Samuels smiled, too. ''I'd say we're all lucky to have another Manford associated with St. Mark's. Of course, one or two of the unattached young nurses may not go along with me on that,'' he added with a sly chuckle.

Megan looked disturbed by this. ''Why not?''

''Because they're jealous, that's why. You've been here only a couple of weeks and already you've snared the attention of our eligible doctors, Hadley and Kane.''

Megan scoffed at this. ''Well, I hardly think that being the cause of a man getting knifed is an endearing way to get his attention. And as for Evan Kane, I only spoke to him for half a minute waiting for the elevator. He probably wouldn't recognize me if he saw me again.'' There was an amused twinkle in her eyes. ''I suggest you tell your eager young nurses to hang in there. It's open season on good-looking, successful, unmarried doctors.'' She grinned mischievously.

''I'll just bet it is,'' he said, arching one eyebrow in a knowing look.

The old doctor's eyes in their deep sockets were wise and understanding. *Not much gets by him,* Megan thought as he turned away. She watched him go out the door, thinking how thoughtful and caring it had been of him to seek her out this morning. Talking with him left her with a warm feeling. His benevolent manner reminded her so much of her father.

Later that week Megan received an interesting telephone call. ''Miss Manford, this is Harold Gallagher with the Claysun Police Department,'' a man's authoritative-sounding voice informed her. ''I think you'll be interested to know that we've taken a man into custody that we've reason to think might be the same one who assaulted you and Dr. Hadley last week.''

''Really?'' The rising inflection in Megan's voice mirrored both surprise and interest.

''Yes, at least there's a possibility. This man robbed a convenience store last night and threatened the clerk with a knife that is similar to the one you described after your attack. And in general he fits the description you gave of the man.''

''I do hope you're right. Everyone around St. Mark's will be greatly relieved if you've caught the man who hurt Dr. Hadley.''

''Well, we'll check that out today if you'll come down and see if you can identify him in a lineup. We'd like it if you could arrange to do that this morning. In fact, that's why I called—to set up a time that's convenient for you. What about eleven or eleven-thirty?''

Megan thought about it for a second and decided to go as late as she could and therefore work it into her lunch hour. ''Eleven-thirty would be good for me,'' she responded amiably. ''And do I just ask for Mr. Gallagher?''

''Better make it Harry,'' he told her with a wry laugh. ''They don't stand much on ceremony in our division.''

When Megan drove away from the hospital shortly after eleven the temperature was one hundred and one degrees, and the heat lay like a thick cloth over the city. In the downtown area she circled several blocks trying to find an empty parking place. She finally got a break when a car pulled out of a spot a block and a half from the police station. The parking meter even had twenty-five minutes left on it, which she thought was probably enough. Yet to be on the safe side she put in more coins to give her an hour.

When she went into the police station, Harry Gallagher came to meet her almost immediately. He looked to be in his mid to late thirties, with implacable male features and brawny muscles beneath his rolled-up shirtsleeves. "This will only take five or ten minutes," he said as he ushered Megan into a room and had her stand in front of a one-way viewing window. "You can see them but they can't see you. I'm sure you understand that." He gave her a reassuring nod. "So take your time and look at each man carefully."

After this brief instruction, he gave the signal and six men were marched into the opposite room and lined up to face the viewing glass. Megan moved closer to the window and stood solemnly, her hands tensed at her sides.

One by one each man stepped forward. Megan shrank back involuntarily when Man Number Four stepped out of the line. A cold knot formed in her stomach at the sight of the sullen scowl on his unshaven face and his glowering eyes that seemed to be looking straight at her. She clenched her hands until her nails hurt her palms, but she didn't utter a word until the last two men had stepped forward and then back into the lineup.

"He's number four," she said tersely, looking toward the detective.

"You feel certain number four is the man who attacked you and Dr. Hadley?" Gallagher asked.

"Yes, he's the one all right. There's absolutely no doubt about that."

"Then that does it, Miss Manford. Thank you for coming down." He gave her a brief nod and a polite smile.

"No need to thank me. I was more than glad to come. You and your department are the ones who deserve all our thanks," she said warmly. "We're all going to feel safer now."

Megan lost no time in leaving. While she had great respect and admiration for law keepers, still, being in the confines of the police station gave her the willies. She walked fast out the door and broke into a light run as she headed down the sidewalk.

"Hey! Are you going to a fire or just have a plane to catch?" Tucker Hadley said, grabbing hold of her arm and running along beside her.

"Neither one," she answered, laughing. "I'm only anxious to get away from here. I just witnessed my first police lineup and it sort of grossed me out."

"I know what you mean. I was there shortly ahead of you. In fact, I saw you go in, so I was waiting for you to finish and come out.''

''Oh . . .'' Her lips made a circle and she looked up at him questioningly. ''Did you identify the man who attacked you?''

''Yeah, he was number four. Did you recognize him?''

She nodded. ''I'll never forget that man's face. He's ugly as galvanized sin.''

Tucker's lips twitched in amusement. ''I've heard of ugly as sin, but *galvanized* sin—that's got to be the ugliest. Right?''

''Right,'' she agreed, having to laugh in spite of herself.

''Okay then. I'd say we've both done our civic duty and identified the criminal. He will now be justly punished. So let's you and I talk about something different and pleasant over lunch. My treat.''

Megan glanced at her wristwatch and sighed. ''I'd like to, Tucker, but I don't have time. I'm due back at the hospital in about thirty-five minutes. I'll have to grab a sandwich on the run.''

''No problem. We can do that together. You know, the Main Street Deli is less than two blocks from here. They've got great sandwiches.''

He didn't wait for her to agree. He simply took a firmer hold on her arm and headed her in the direction of Main Street. By the time they entered the deli they had discussed what kind of sandwich they each wanted, and both of them settled on corned beef on rye with potato salad on the side. They also opted for glasses of iced sun tea, which was a summertime specialty of the deli.

''I feel like I'm back in school,'' Megan said as she slipped into one of the wooden chairs with a notebook-size desk arm on which she could set her food.

''I see what you mean,'' Tucker concurred, taking the chair next to hers.

''I bet these sturdy old chairs came from one of those Claysun Board of Education renovation sales.''

''In that case I intend to look them over and see if some boyfriend of yours carved your initials joined in a heart with his. I bet plenty of guys had a crush on Megan Manford. Right?''

She angled her head at him, a teasing glint in her eyes. ''I'd say there was more than one but fewer than six,'' she answered facetiously. ''And in my days of wild, mad youth the guys were more inclined to billboard graffiti than initials carved into wooden chairs. So I doubt if you'll find 'John loves Megan' carved anyplace.'' Having said this, Megan felt this trivial bit of conversation between them was surely ended. She concentrated her full attention on the lunch before her by taking a man-sized bite of her sandwich.

There was silence now between them as they ate. Megan finished off her potato salad and was drinking some tea before eating the other half of her sandwich when Tucker glanced inquiringly at her. "Does this John still love you, Megan?" he asked.

He sounded totally serious, and Megan stared at him, unable to believe he was picking up this silly topic of conversation again. "There is no John. Not back then and not now, Tucker. I just used the name as an example in our fun kind of talk about old high school chairs."

"If there's no John, then I'm wondering if there is someone who's important to you. Are you involved now, Megan?" he asked, his expression stilled and entirely serious.

His question took her by complete surprise. Why was Tucker asking her this? They hardly knew each other. Surely it couldn't matter to him whether she was involved in a relationship or not. She eyed him quizzically. "You know I've just started a new job with the hospital. I'm involved with my work, Tucker. That's what's of major importance to me right now."

He tilted his brow, looking at her uncertainly. "That doesn't answer my question." For a moment he studied her intently. "Is there a man in your life—someone special?"

Megan didn't know why, but she hesitated to give Tucker a direct answer. "Well, now, let's see." She paused as if giving the matter serious thought. "There's a cute guy who delivers the newspaper each morning. He's skinny as a flute and only about fourteen years old. Then there's this mechanic where I take my car. He's a big bear of a man, always wears green coveralls and a red baseball cap. He's a whiz with motor noises and fuel pumps. Trouble is he's pushing fifty and has a wife and three kids. 'Course, today I met this nice-looking Detective Gallagher. He seemed a little special, but then Mother cautioned me about three kinds of men, and a policeman was one of them." She thought Tucker would find her flippant answer funny and laugh, but all he did was shake his head at her with an enigmatic smile marking his lips.

"I'm probably a fool to ask, but what were the other two your mother warned you about?"

"Butchers and doctors," she said without a second's hesitation. Then laughter floated up from her throat.

Tucker's sense of humor took over and he laughed in answer. "I walked right into that one, didn't I?" he said, grimacing. "You really know how to discourage a guy, you know that? What does it take to get a simple yes or no answer out of you, anyway? I simply wanted to find out if you were attached or not, 'cause if you're not I was going to ask you to go sailing with me this week-end.''

When she heard this, Megan's eyebrows shot up in interest while a smile lit up her eyes in an in-credible way. ''No, and yes,'' she responded im-mediately. ''How's that for a simple answer?''

''No and yes both. That confuses me.''

''No, I'm not attached, and yes, I'd love to go sailing with you.'' She said the words with cer-tainty, her voice velvet-edged.

He smiled his mercurial smile. ''You've got yourself a date to sail Sunday afternoon with me at Cedar Lake then, Megan. You'll have to help me out some when two hands are needed. I'm lim-ited with what I can manage with this one banged-up arm. However, most things I can handle with this good, strong, undamaged right arm of mine,'' he bragged, making a fist and raising his right arm in a power salute.

''I can be your left arm, Tucker. In fact I wel-come the chance. You helped me when I needed it; now it's my turn.'' There was a depth to her smile as she said this, and her mouth curved with tenderness thinking of the debt she owed him.

He gazed at her and beamed approval. ''I'd like

nothing better than to have you as my partner working beside me,'' he said. And as they looked at each other a vaguely sensuous light passed between them. . . .

Chapter Three

When Megan awoke Sunday morning she looked around her bedroom, involuntarily squinting at the bright daggers of sunlight piercing the edges of the curtains. It was going to be another extremely hot day. Thank goodness she was getting away from the city. Surely it would be somewhat cooler at Cedar Lake. Didn't they say that a body of water had a moderating influence on weather?

She stretched her arms up over her head, making little contented noises not unlike those of a purring kitten. She was thinking about the day that lay ahead and her date to go sailing with Tucker. She thought about the circumstances that had led up to

Tucker asking her to come with him today. All their foolish talk that got started because of those old-style desk chairs that provided the only seating at the Main Street Deli. It had been pretty silly, all of it, but rather fun, too. She chuckled inwardly, recalling the ''John loves Megan'' bit she'd concocted. She scrambled out of bed thinking that the oddest part was the way Tucker latched on to that and maneuvered it into a discussion of whether she was currently seeing someone or not.

Heading for the shower, she couldn't help but wonder if Tucker's asking her to accompany him sailing had been a spur-of-the-moment idea. Or if he'd had it in mind all along, and that's why he hung around the police station until she came out, then suggested they grab a quick lunch. Had he made it all seem impromptu so he could ask her out in such a casual way that she wouldn't think it was a big deal or anything? She frowned, thinking that it made sense with what Dr. Samuels had implied. If the pretty nurses were eyeing Tucker, vying for his favor and attention, he could be leery of her, too.

''Well, doctor, that's fine and dandy with me,'' Megan told herself, adjusting the water temperature and stepping into the shower stall. She had no designs on Tucker and she'd make sure he realized that an afternoon sail was not a bona fide date.

Actually, it was more of a friendly get-together of two people interested in the same sport.

Tucker telephoned while she was showering and left a message on her answering machine. ''I'm taking sunscreen lotion for both of us, but Megan, you'll need some sort of hat and had better wear something that will give you protection from the sun. You can get a nasty sunburn out there on the water, you know.''

Heeding Tucker's warning, she decided against wearing shorts, opting instead for white cotton slacks with a T-shirt and tennis shoes. She rummaged around through her things to locate a blue-and-white billed cap that had the Greek letters of her sorority across the front, part of the memorabilia from her college days.

It had been several years since Megan had made a trip to Cedar Lake. Now with Tucker doing the driving, she relaxed in the front seat beside him, gazing out the window at the countryside. The low rolling hills were dotted with blackjack oak and native pecan trees and the smaller picturesque red-buds and dogwoods. Nearer the road there were scattered patches of black-eyed Susan, bushy yellow thistlepoppy, and lots of chickweed with deeply notched white petals that would develop into papery capsules containing small seeds that songbirds relished.

There was a fair amount of traffic, but they made good time. Less than an hour after they left Claysun they were following the natural wild beauty of the shoreline, viewing the deep-pink rose mallow blooms that looked like miniature holly-hocks, and knotweeds with their slender clusters of small pink flowers. The rather large, dark seeds of knotweeds were choice foods of waterfowl and game birds.

They soon arrived at the marina. Tucker hurried Megan down to the cove where the sailboats were docked. "There she is," Tucker cried, pointing out a white boat with the block letters ET painted in black on the stern. "What do you think of her?"

"Oh my, Tucker, she's trim and truly fair," she said, her voice rising in her enthusiasm.

"She's that, all right. I'm glad you approve of Evan's and my dream boat." He grinned at her, obviously pleased that Megan shared his excite-ment in the boat. "Evan and I are joint owners. That's why she's named *ET*. E for Evan and T for Tucker. Clever, huh?"

She laughed. "Certainly very appropriate, at least. I was afraid there for a minute that you were one of those space freaks, and that *ET* might stand for extraterrestrial."

"Nope. I'm strictly a land and sea man. I'm only interested in the winsome beauties right here on earth, and those enticing mermaids who inhabit the water.''

''I seriously doubt you'll find a mermaid in Cedar Lake,'' she told him, amusement glistening in her eyes.

''That's okay with me. A lady with a fishtail can't hold a candle to a gal with a great pair of legs anyway.''

''Is that something you learned from your anatomy course, Doctor?'' she asked, a mocking smile now playing at the corners of her lips.

''No, from keen observation,'' Tucker countered, giving her shapely figure a slow, careful head-to-toe appraisal, and then beaming his approval.

''Cut the comedy and stop leering at me, Tucker,'' she protested, placing her hands on her hips pugnaciously. ''We did come here to sail, so don't you think it's time we got started?''

''Right,'' Tucker agreed, leaping into the boat, and then holding his hand out to her to help her aboard.

For the next several minutes they talked little. Megan offered her assistance in stepping the mast, and they worked together rigging the sails. In fairly short order they were under way.

The sun was a brilliant blaze reflecting brightly off the surface of the blue-green water. At

Tucker's insistence Megan smoothed suntan oil on her arms and her throat and neck. Then she donned her dark glasses and squared her cap so the bill would shade the upper part of her face.

Settling down now to relax and enjoy an afternoon of sailing, Megan sat with her legs tucked under her and watched Tucker handling the boat. They sailed for a while at a short distance from the shore. At one point they passed by a number of anglers fishing for bass where there was a thick base of willow trees growing at the edge of the water. A few minutes later as they sailed around an outjutting point of land, the wind picked up and filled the sails. Now Tucker headed the *ET* into the center of the lake.

''Tell me about your sailboat, Tucker. How long have you and Evan been sailing here on Cedar Lake?'' Megan asked, transferring her gaze from the billowing sails to admire Tucker's tanned hand gripping the tiller.

''About three years now.''

''And do the two of you find the time to sail fairly often?''

''Not quite as often as we'd both like,'' he said with a faint shrug. ''However, at that, we manage to hoist the sails more regularly than I ever figured we would when we decided to take the plunge and indulge ourselves in a neat boat like this one.''

There was a look of sheer contentment on Tucker's broad suntanned face that let Megan know that he'd never regretted this indulgence for even a second. "And do you and Evan usually sail the *ET* together—just the two of you?"

Tucker nodded. "Most of the time we do. On a couple of occasions, though, Evan brought the girl he goes with along. He's trying to get her interested in sailing, but she's very uncomfortable on the water. She can't swim, so she gets uneasy if we take the boat out too far from the shore."

"Doesn't wearing a life preserver give her the reassurance she needs? That and having two bold athletic men with her to handle any emergency? That should be inducement enough for any true-blue American girl."

"Well, it wasn't for this afternoon, at least. Evan wanted to bring Linda and join us, but she vetoed the idea. They are going to meet us at the Shanty Hut for dinner, though. I hope that's all right with you."

"It's more than all right. It sounds like great fun." Megan's highly enthusiastic tone of voice echoed her pleased reaction to his plan. "You hadn't told me that supper was to be a part of our Sunday outing," she added rather coyly.

He gave her a wry look. "You didn't think I'd take you back home hungry, surely."

"To be honest I didn't think about it one way or the other."

"Then let me assure you that I intend this to be a first-class date, Megan." His eyes brightened with merriment. "We're going to have a pleasurable afternoon sail, followed by a nice catfish dinner at the Shanty Hut." He leaned his head closer to hers, looking her straight in the eyes. "You do like fried catfish, don't you?"

She bobbed her head affirmatively. "Of course I do."

"And how do you feel about hush puppies?"

"They're an absolute must with fried catfish," she declared emphatically.

"My thought exactly. Now one more question," he continued, his eyes sparkling as though he was playing a game. "Depending what fruits are in season around here, Shanty Hut has great homemade pies. Are you ready for a piece of fresh blueberry pie?"

She observed him with her sweet musing look. "My answer depends on you."

"It does? How's that?"

A smile ruffled her mouth. "I'm ready for blueberry pie if you're ready to sit across the table from a gal with blue teeth."

Tucker threw his head back, laughing. "I think I'll recommend that you try their fresh peach pie.

And for the same reason I'll pass up those blue-
berries and take the peach, too.''

"Well, now that we're in total agreement on a
dinner menu, I'd like you to tell me about your
friend Evan. It makes for a nicer party if you can
know a little about the people ahead of time. Don't
you think?'' She still sat cross-legged, but as she
spoke she stretched her legs out in front of her and
leaned backward and balanced on the palms of her
hands.

"You saw Evan at the hospital, so you know
he's a tall, lean, rusty-haired guy about my age.
He's a good doctor, probably almost as good as I
am,'' Tucker boasted facetiously. "Beyond that,
he's an excellent diagnostician, and in that area,
I'll have to admit, he's better than I am. I'm convinced that's his sixth sense.''

"That's quite an endorsement of your colleague.''

"Evan's more than a colleague. He's a friend
without equal. The finest friend I could ever
have.'' Tucker said the words with immutable cer-
tainty.

"Sounds like your friendship goes back a long
way. Did you and Evan grow up in the same town
together?'' she asked, contemplating Tucker with
eager interest. She wanted to pursue this conver-

sation further on the chance that she'd learn more about Tucker. She'd love to hear about his family and what he'd been like growing up. She wondered what made him decide he wanted to be a doctor.

''No, we're both from different states. Our paths didn't cross until we got into medical school. After that we interned together, then took our residency at the same hospital down in Houston.'' He paused, a pensive expression marking his face. ''Those were grueling years. Makes me bone-weary just thinking about them. But there's a lot of good to be said for that time, too. We acquired the skills and knowledge of well-trained physicians, and Evan and I formed a friendship that will last a lifetime. Neither of us could ask for more than that.'' Tucker stated all this emphatically.

There was an inherent strength in his face as he spoke. Megan regarded him with a speculative look, taking satisfaction in studying his compelling blue eyes, his firm features, and the confident set of his shoulders. *This is no ordinary man,* Megan thought. In fact at this moment she was experiencing a vital awareness of his special qualities. Qualities that she found both admirable and endearing.

The slanting rays of the sun, stark and pitiless, fell on Tucker's face. He wiped the back of his hand across his damp forehead. He came about, changing the boat's direction, and sailed in a long reach back across the lake.

Megan and Tucker didn't attempt to talk much now. Instead they sat relaxed and quiet as the sailboat whispered through the water. The sun sank lower and lower, and long shafts of yellow light stabbed at the waves, and soon blue shadows lay in pools on the low hills across the harbor.

"What time are we to meet Evan and Linda?" Megan asked, when she realized the course of the *ET* was now directed toward the marina.

"I told him we'd be there at seven."

Megan looked at her wristwatch and frowned. "Do you know that it's already six o'clock?" She took off her cap and ran her fingers through her wind-tossed hair. "I really need to clean up a little before we go to the Shanty Hut. Is there someplace I can do that?" Her frown deepened and she heaved a worried sigh. "I'm a windblown mess, and I smell like a mixture of cocoa butter and baby oil." She made a face at him. "What's in this suntan cream of yours, anyway?"

"All the right stuff to preserve that lovely skin of yours," he said, in his professional doctor-to-patient tone of voice. "I only prescribe what's in the best interest for any patient," Tucker added, swallowing a smile to maintain a straight face.

"It may be good for me. But you have to admit it doesn't exactly smell like Chanel Number Five."

"How can I tell, when you're staying so far away from me? Now if you'll come here and sit close to me so I can nuzzle your ear I'll be only too happy to define the scent." His eyes didn't waver from hers, and his gaze was soft as a caress.

Megan knew he was only teasing her. Still, it was a definite thrill, causing her to feel a lurch of excitement within her. She cleared her throat, pretending not to be affected. "There's no time for silliness. You concentrate on sailing the *ET* to the dock, and finding me a place where I can wash up for dinner," she said with quiet firmness. "Can you do that for me—please?" she added quickly.

"I can do that easily, and I'm happy to," he said warmly. "I'd be happy to do most anything at all for you, Megan." He smiled at her, his eyes humorous and tender.

It was at that moment that Megan sensed that an undeniable magnetism was building between them.

Chapter Four

The Shanty Hut was aptly named. It was a small, square structure that had been painted chocolate brown, however not too recently. Its dark, weathered exterior was given a bright touch by the addition of decorative shutters in the same tangerine color as the entrance door.

"Well, what do you know? Looks like we beat 'em here," Tucker announced as he parked in a place right in front of the restaurant. "And we're right on time, too." He pointed to the digital clock on the dashboard. "See, seven o'clock straight up."

"What makes you think they're not already here?"

"I don't see Evan's car, that's why."

She frowned at him. "I saw a number of cars parked along the side of the building as we drove in. Maybe his is there."

Tucker shook his head. "No way." He scoffed. "Evan believes in parking as close to an entrance as he can get. You see those three openings just opposite the front door? If he was here he'd be parked in one of those. Believe me."

The words were scarcely out of Tucker's mouth before a shiny black sports car wheeled into a parking space two cars away from Tucker and Megan. The next moment Tucker and Evan were greeting each other and introducing Megan and Linda as the four of them entered the Shanty Hut together.

Megan was pleased to see that the inside of the restaurant was brighter and more interesting than the nondescript exterior. The walls were painted a creamy white and were decorated with several attractively framed pictures of southwestern-style landscapes. There were booths around three sides of the square-shaped room. All were upholstered in a persimmon-colored vinyl and the tabletops were jet-black Formica.

Evan quickly spotted a corner booth and immediately steered Linda and Megan toward it. "You girls slide into the middle. Tucker and I will sit at each end," he directed, arranging the seating so he was by Linda and Tucker beside Megan.

Linda slipped into the semicircular booth first. As she took her designated spot the soft glow of the ceiling lights made a halo of her wheat-colored hair that framed her cameo-pretty face.

"What did you think of the *ET*?" Evan asked Megan once all four of them had unanimously agreed to order the fried catfish dinner.

"She's great!" Megan exclaimed. "We had a good sail, didn't we, Tucker?" She cast an enthusiastic smile in Tucker's direction. "We caught a breeze once we were out in the middle of the lake that gave us a perfect sail."

"That's good. How did Tucker manage with his injured shoulder without me to aid him?" A serious, questioning expression tightened Evan's mouth.

"Very well, I'd say. I helped a little with the sails, but other than that Tucker did it all. And did it masterfully, I might add."

Evan shot an amused look at Tucker. "I've got to hand it to you, Tuck. One afternoon of sailing and you've got Megan almost ready to believe that you could sail in the America's Cup Race with one arm tied behind your back." A low ripple of laughter came from deep in his throat.

Tucker grinned good-naturedly. "All I did was

give it my best shot so Megan will want to sail with me again next week.'' He reached over and covered Megan's hand with his as he said this. ''Do you think you might like to do this again next weekend with me, Megan?'' he asked, his smile holding all the charm that came so naturally to him when he wanted to use it.

Her merry eyes looked warmly into his as she answered. ''I think it would be nice if maybe all four of us did something together.''

''I think so, too,'' Linda interjected. ''Tucker and Evan could take us sailing; you and I, Megan, could bring along a picnic lunch. We'd have a fun time, the four of us.'' She spoke in an animated rush of words. Then looking at Evan, her violet eyes dancing with excitement, she said, ''Let's all go sailing on the *ET*. We could do that, couldn't we, Evan?''

Megan looked at Linda in utter disbelief. After what Tucker had told her of Linda's anxieties about being out on the water, she was more than a little surprised to hear her eagerly instigating a sailing excursion and picnic.

Obviously Tucker was even more amazed than Megan. He gaped like an oyster. ''Is Linda really serious about this?'' He directed his question to Evan.

''She sounds like it to me,'' he said, smiling and

giving Linda a conspiratorial wink. "I think now's the time to tell Tucker what you've been up to, Linda."

"I've been taking swimming lessons," she announced, sounding well pleased with herself. "And every weekend all summer Evan has been swimming with me and making me become a strong, confident swimmer. He's worked so long and hard with me that I'm afraid I've worn him completely out." She gave Evan a look of affectionate concern. "In fact, I made him stop doing laps with me this afternoon because he looked unusually tired and his face was so pale it worried me."

Tucker shot a critical look at Evan. "You really don't look all that great, my friend. You could have a little iron-deficiency anemia." A disturbed frown seemed to shadow Tucker's keen eyes.

"Knock it off, folks. We're all here to eat catfish together, not to hear clinical evaluations of my paleness. If you'll stop and think about it a minute, you'll remember that people with bright-red hair like mine characteristically have very white skin that freckles and sunburns." He paused and gave Megan his friendly, off-center smile. "Now Megan, on the other hand, has red hair, but it's dark mahogany red with a lot of brown in it. She's lucky because with that you get a warm creamy skin that will even suntan if she's careful about the amount of sun she gets.'' His smile moved to his eyes and he looked at Megan with tender affection. ''You know, you remind me so much of what I remember about my mother. She had hair exactly the same color as yours, and she was pretty like you are, too.''

''That's out-and-out flattery, but I like it.'' Megan laughed and turned to Linda. ''Red hair and charm, too—he's a keeper. You hang on to him, Linda.''

''I just might try to do that,'' she replied, as some private emotion glistened in her eyes and her laughter became musically husky.

Their talking ceased momentarily, for their waiter was approaching them, ready to serve their dinner. He was almost completely bald, and he wore a perpetual smile like a fluorescent light that was never turned off. He looked to be just past fifty. He was a little hunched, shoulders and arms rounded as though to shake hands, head inclined in the classic stance of the professional host. Observing him, Megan surmised that in his better days he probably had been headwaiter in a classy restaurant somewhere, for he served their catfish with as much flourish as if it were chateaubriand.

The catfish had been dipped in a well-seasoned batter and cooked to perfection, and the golden-brown hush puppies had to be the best Megan had ever tasted. Apparently they all agreed with her, for everybody promptly began to eat with obvious gusto. Lighthearted conversation bounded back and forth between the four of them during the meal. Evan appeared to relax; he even looked less weary and pale than he had earlier. Linda was effervescent. Tucker wore an expression of complete satisfaction, as if he took full credit for bringing about this harmonious evening. Looking at all of them, Megan smiled inwardly. She felt she saw what Tucker was also seeing, that in a very short period of time these friends of his had become a companionable foursome.

"I hate to break up the party," Evan said when they'd finished their pie and coffee. "But it's an hour's drive back to Claysun, and it's getting late."

"Yeah, and tomorrow is a workday for all of us," Linda added, laying her napkin on the table and sliding over to join Evan as he got out of the booth.

Tucker and Megan followed suit, and while the fellows were taking care of the check Megan asked Linda about her job. "I work for the law firm of Shelton, Graham and Burkwald," she answered. "I'm a legal secretary for Maurice Burkwald."

A second later the two couples stepped outside

into the warm summer night and headed for their cars. There was only the slightest breeze stirring, yet the darkness made the air seem cooler. The night was full of summer sounds, the guttural croak of frogs and the high-pitched droning of the cicada. That broad-headed insect with prominent eyes and two pairs of membranous wings had fascinated Megan as a child. She remembered when she was growing up that her father would sometimes take her with him when he went out for a walk after dinner. On those warm July and August nights the humming song of the cicadas was heard everywhere they walked. Maybe that was the reason that she still found the sound pleasant to hear. It brought back happy childhood memories.

As Megan and Tucker started on the drive back to Claysun, the darkness was thick and warm as blue velvet. Overhead the many stars were like shards of glittering silver, their constellations etched across the night sky with startling clarity, while the moon simply formed a slender ivory crescent.

''You know what? I still can't get over all that about Linda taking swimming lessons, and working hard all summer to get over her fear of the water,'' Tucker said, breaking into Megan's quiet reverie. ''Before tonight, I took her for a timid sort, apprehensive about most everything. I guess something happened that brought about a change in her.''

"Not something, but *someone*. Evan happened to her,'' Megan said, wrapping her words in a knowing smile. ''She wants to please him by being able to enjoy all the same things that he does. That includes sailing on the *ET*.''

"You think that's it?'' He cocked his head at her questioningly.

Megan laughed. ''I know darn well it is. Just think about it a minute. I bet you've had a woman or two who's gone to some effort to do the same for you, now haven't you?''

He gave an indifferent shrug. ''Nobody put out time and money on lessons in order to swim, sail, or play golf with me that I know of.''

"Well, that only proves that you've dated water nymphs and low handicappers,'' she quipped, taunting him with her teasing tone.

Evidently Tucker had no comeback to this. He simply tossed Megan a noncommittal half smile and concentrated his attention on driving. Megan lapsed into silence, too. They drove for several miles, both of them engaged in their own quiet thoughts.

"You know what?'' Tucker asked, suddenly coming out of his apparent reverie. ''I think Evan surprised me more than Linda did tonight.''

''What do you mean?'' Megan leaned forward, a look of interest sharpening her expression.

''Well, I know Evan better than almost anyone, and he's not a guy who usually talks about himself, or anything personal. But evidently you struck a chord within him, because tonight is the only time I ever heard him mention what his mother looked like.'' Tucker did not look at her; rather, he narrowed his eyes pensively, staring straight ahead into the darkness. ''It seems an odd thing for him to do.''

''What happened to his mother?'' she asked.

''Both his parents died after their home was struck by a tornado,'' Tucker said tersely.

Shocked by hearing this, Megan shook her head sadly. ''That's so terrible. Poor Evan—was he badly hurt?''

''No. Fortunately he wasn't home. He'd gone four blocks away to the birthday party of one of the kids in his first-grade class.'' Tucker paused, his lips pursed in thought. ''You know, when you're only six years old it's easy to blame yourself when something bad happens. And to a degree I think Evan did this.''

Megan looked puzzled. ''What do you mean? How could any child possibly think a natural disaster is in any way his fault?''

"If his parents die and he has to deal with that at six years of age, he could. At any rate, Evan did. For some odd reason he blamed himself for what happened. He felt that if he hadn't gone to the birthday party and had been home with his folks when the tornado struck he could have done something to save them."

Megan looked distressed, a frown etching lines across her forehead. "That's a lot of painful baggage for a little boy to carry. I hope there was some family to help him get through it."

Tucker nodded. "There was. Evan had an aunt and uncle in New Mexico. They took him to live with them."

"That's a happier note. I'm glad there was someone there for him."

A few minutes later Megan saw that they had reached the Silverline River. Ahead of them cars moved on the bridge like beetles under the blue glare of the sodium lights. In the distance the lights of Claysun floated like fireworks in the darkness.

Soon they were driving along the parkway near Megan's house. "I'm sorry this evening has come to an end," Tucker said, as he walked Megan to her front door. "I don't want to wait clear until next weekend's picnic outing and sail before I see you again. So can we do something together the middle of the week, do you think, say Wednesday?"

Her mouth curved into an unconscious smile. ''I think Wednesday would be very nice.''

''Good,'' he said, tilting her chin with the tips of his fingers so he could look into her eyes. She knew he was going to kiss her, and she didn't want to stop him. Her eyes closed of their own accord as she waited. His lips, when they touched hers, were soft, giving as well as taking, persuading her gently to respond. She could feel his arms cradle her against him. He felt strong, and she felt safe and natural in his embrace. His fingers touching her face were tender, trailing whispery shadows over her cheekbones. Having him kiss her felt like the most natural thing in the world. It was a sweet kiss, a tender gesture, tempting an answer but demanding none. ''Good night, Megan. Sleep well,'' he whispered against her hair. And then he was gone.

Chapter Five

Megan went inside her house, but she didn't close the front door until the sound of Tucker's car pulling out of her drive had faded away. It was late, and her common sense told her she should hike upstairs to her bedroom and start getting ready for bed, not stand starry-eyed in the front hall thinking silly, romantic thoughts because Tucker's good-night kiss had thrown her off her equilibrium.

She had known men like Tucker before. Good men who were friendly, dependable, interesting, and attractive. But none of them had stirred her deeper feelings. Now it seemed a man had come along whose smile could make her heart start racing, and whose touch sent delicious shivers down her spine. She sighed, still staring at the ceiling.

The heirloom hall clock chimed the quarter hour. Megan began to climb the stairs, telling herself that she'd obviously become light-headed from being out in the sun too long on the *ET*. Why else would she be rhapsodizing over a simple kiss? After all, it was nothing more or less than a friendly way for a couple to part after sharing a pleasant time together.

With determined steps Megan marched into her bedroom, undressed quickly, and stepped into the shower. She pushed other thoughts from her mind, intent now on shampooing her hair and then lathering on fragrant jasmine-scented soap to wash off the residue of suntan oil that Tucker had insisted she use while they were sailing.

At first the water was too hot, so she turned the cold-water tap. That felt good. She began to relax. After she'd washed her hair, she stood under the shower for some time, playing back the various aspects of this day through her mind. She knew now that Tucker had planned for them to join Evan and Linda after they'd finished sailing. She wondered why he hadn't told her that at the very beginning. Surely he couldn't have thought she'd object to their making it a foursome. Actually she'd liked the idea very much. Certainly it had worked out. The four of them hit it off famously.

Now that she had time to think about it, she was beginning to understand why Tucker had talked so much about Evan. Evan was his best friend, and apparently it was important to Tucker that she get to really know and like him. Tucker must have told her all he had about Evan's background so she could appreciate his complexities, and see just where he was coming from. It gave her a good feeling that Tucker had shared Evan's history with her. Her intuition told her that Tucker had never discussed this with anyone else but her. She couldn't help but wonder just how significant that might prove to be.

Megan turned off the water and stepped out of the shower. As soon as she'd wrapped a towel into a turban around her wet hair, she grabbed up another to dry herself. Her mind was still churning over the day's happenings. Thinking back to their dinner at the Shanty Hut, Megan couldn't believe how she'd immediately felt at ease with Evan and Linda. Usually it took her a while to feel really comfortable with new acquaintances, but she'd felt an instant rapport with Linda, and, like Tucker had said, she did seem to strike a chord within Evan. Probably because he somehow sensed that she wanted to help ease the situation for him that arose when the others brought up the subject of his pallor and weariness.

What had been wrong with Linda and Tucker? Why weren't they aware that what they said really bothered Evan? He'd gone into that lengthy explanation about the shades of red hair and the complexions that went with them as a screen. After all, no man liked to be told he appears tired and wan, particularly by the woman he's obviously in love with. Megan had felt Evan's distress so keenly. Why had the two people who knew him the best and cared the most about him failed to see it at all?

Megan slept restlessly, waking often to hear traffic dwindle as the night deepened, and hear it start again as black turned to gray, and then she finally glimpsed a row of misty dawn light between the slats of the miniblinds. She lifted her head up off the pillow. What was that she was hearing? It sounded like the gentle whispering sound of rain falling through the trees. Could it be that Claysun's long, hot, dry spell was broken at last?

Without taking time to locate her slippers, she ran barefoot across her bedroom, opening the blinds to welcome the sight of the fat, clumsy raindrops that were rolling down the windowpanes, as well as the peculiarly lovely crystalline light that rain made in a room.

It was early, for she'd awakened well before her alarm clock buzzer went off. She dressed, ate a leisurely breakfast, even had time to do the crossword puzzle in the morning paper.

Outside now the skies were clearing. As she drove to work, car tires hummed along the wet streets, spewing water like whale spray where the wheels hit puddles left by the rain. She had the radio on in the car and it was playing the song about laughter in the rain that she'd always liked. The lilting melody stayed with her, and she found herself still singing the refrain in a muted voice as she sat down in front of the computer to get to work.

Megan was busy all morning, a usual Monday after the weekend, with people coming in with various requests for data, and several brief interruptions. Right before noon she had three telephone calls in succession.

"Records, Megan Manford," she answered the last call tersely.

"Hi, Megan," Tucker's voice was bright and chipper. "Bet I called you at a hectic time. Did I?"

"Yeah, sort of. Mondays invariably get that

way.'' She didn't want to sound like she was putting him off, so she quickly added, ''But you're a nice diversion. I'm glad you called.''

''I like hearing I'm a nice diversion,'' he said warmly, sounding pleased. ''So let me divert you further with something I want to ask you.''

''Ask away.'' She laughed into the phone, wanting to show that her good nature was back.

''Well, since the rain cooled things off a speck, it shouldn't be too uncomfortable to be outside tonight. I hoped I could talk you into going to the ball game with me.''

Mystified, Megan hesitated a moment before she answered. ''What sort of ball game are we talking about?''

''Baseball, of course. You do know our Claysun Drillers are number two in the league, don't you?''

''Sorry, Tucker, but I'm not into baseball. To be absolutely truthful, I've never attended a baseball game.''

''You're kidding!'' He sounded as astonished as if she'd told him she'd never been to the circus. ''Let me tell you something, Honey. You don't know what you've missed,'' Tucker declared emphatically.

''No, I don't.'' Megan laughed. ''But I'm sure you're going to show me.''

* * *

After the rain the evening air was mild and there was a faint breeze. Tucker made sure that they got to the ballpark well before the first ball was thrown out, telling Megan that he wanted her to experience the ambience surrounding the ball game from start to finish. The smells of popcorn, peanuts, nachos, and hot dogs hovered in the air near the concession stand. The bleachers were rapidly filling up with the crowd of laughing, talking, noisy fans, many of whom sported kelly-green baseball caps to show they were here to root for the home team.

"I'd say this is one big, happy, enthusiastic gathering. Is it usually like this?" Megan asked as she and Tucker located a good place to sit.

"Sure is. And it gets even more so once the game gets under way. Baseball is called the great American pastime, you know," he said, teasing her with a wry grin.

"So I've been told," she countered with a grimace. "But I'll need you to explain the fine points as the game goes along so I can truly appreciate it," she added good-naturedly.

"Can do," Tucker replied, and immediately began explaining the rules as the first inning got under way.

The visiting team was up to bat and their first two batters walked. A close play at first base brought part of the crowd to its feet. ''Hey, he was out!'' one fan shouted at the umpire.

''Bad call!'' another yelled.

Megan shot a confused look at Tucker. ''Why the fuss? He looked like he was safe to me.''

Tucker nodded, agreeing. ''He was. If he hadn't been, the umpire would have reversed the call.''

During the next inning while the Claysun team was up at bat, Tucker directed Megan's attention to the other team's pitcher. ''Watch him now. He's sure to throw high outside next.''

''Why would he do that?''

''Because our batter swung at his last pitch. He'll throw this one, you'll see.''

''You're telling me he'll just throw a ball intentionally? Why?''

''Because it's smart to mix up your pitches. If you keep throwing strikes all the time, they hit you out of the ballpark. The good pitchers throw a mix.''

''And here I thought they stretched their arms and went through all that windup rigmarole to baffle the poor batters.''

Tucker laughed. ''That's only in the movies, Megan.''

He continued to explain things to her and as the innings flew by Megan became totally caught up in the game. The score remained close, but at the middle of the ninth inning the visitors were ahead by one run. The Claysun Drillers now came up for their final time at bat. Things went well for them, however, and with the bases loaded the visiting team blew their chance for a double play when the shortstop bobbled the ball and Claysun scored a run. The score was now tied. Then the next batter struck out, but the runner on third stole home on an overthow, giving Claysun the winning point. Zealous fans went wild in jubilation, and this included Tucker and Megan, of course.

''Your very first baseball game and your team wins. This calls for a celebration,'' Tucker said as they climbed down from the bleachers and headed for Tucker's car. ''How about going to the Sweet Shoppe and getting a chocolate sundae with extra nuts, lots of whipped cream, and two maraschino cherries?''

She widened her eyes, feigning a look of horror. ''You're a doctor and you're suggesting we eat something with all that fat and cholesterol? I shudder just thinking about what that could do to our arteries.'' She emphasized her words dramatically.

He made a sour face. ''You're a spoilsport and something of a health nut to boot.'' He lifted his hands and shoulders in a shrug of resignation. ''But you make a valid point. So I'll scratch the sundae and take you to the Coffee House for espresso.'' He placed an arm around her waist, and adjusting his steps to match hers, they walked shoulder to shoulder out of the ballpark.

During the following weeks, Megan quite willingly attended all the home ball games with Tucker. And Evan and Linda joined them one night in August for a double-header. The four of them also sailed together on the *ET* when they could arrange it. Over the long Labor Day weekend, they sailed, picnicked, and also took in the holiday dinner dance at the Cedar Lake Boat Club together.

''We four need to give ourselves a name,'' Linda said, while the small dance band took their first intermission and the four of them sat talking together at their table. ''We have such good times together and we should call ourselves something special. How about the Beauties and the Beasts?'' she suggested with a playful gleam in her eyes. ''I think that might fit us. What do you think, Evan?''

He scowled at her. ''Beauties fits you and Megan all right. But Tucker and I resent the label of Beasts. We're not hairy and ugly.''

''No, we're not,'' Tucker instantly agreed. ''We're clean shaven and stouthearted.'' He clenched his fists and flexed his arms to show off his muscles. "I think we should be the Braves and the Broads."

It was Linda's turn to wrinkle her nose in distaste. "You look like a poster for *The Terminator*," she told him with disdain. "I don't like the idea of brute force, and besides that, 'broads' is not a complimentary term."

"Okay—okay," Evan intervened. "I think we should go for something more gallant. How about the Four Musketeers?"

Megan was quick to shake her head at this. "I'm sorry, Evan, but that's sounds strictly male to me. Makes us sound like soldiers in arms." She kept shaking her head and frowning thoughtfully. "If you're really serious about a name for us, then I think we should call ourselves something that shows we're truly very close friends—sort of like family." She hesitated a second. "I know!" she exclaimed, her eyes flashing with excitement. "Cousins. That's what we could call ourselves. We're like four close-knit, friendly, caring cousins."

"You bet we are," Evan agreed wholeheartedly. "I like it. It fits us like a warm mitten." His broad smile not only made his eyes sparkle, but it put a glow of color on his pale cheeks. "What do you think, Linda?" He turned his attention to her, taking hold of her hand. "This was all your idea, so you get the final say. Do you think we should call ourselves Cousins?''

''Absolutely,'' she said, with an agreeing bob of her head. ''If Tucker goes along with it, that is.''

''Sure I do. So it's unanimous. We are now and forevermore the Cousins.'' Tucker stood up and held his hand out to Megan. ''And now that we've settled that important matter, and I see that the band's come back, let's all us cousins get to dancing.''

Megan took Tucker's hand, lacing her fingers with his. ''That was all nice and fun, but I'm not sure I know what brought it all on,'' she said as they stepped onto the dance floor. ''Do you think Linda was playing a game with us?''

''No, I think there was something more to it than that.''

''You do. What, exactly?''

''I think Linda is rather an insecure person. Haven't you sensed that about her?''

''I suppose I have,'' Megan answered hesitantly. ''She's reserved at times, and certainly not very assertive.''

''She needs someone to lean on, I think. Of course, she needs and depends on Evan, and she's certainly blossomed lately, knowing how much Evan cares about her.'' Tucker spoke with authority; obviously he knew that Evan was serious about Linda. "But Linda needs more. I'd say that she desperately needs to feel she belongs, and that she's wholeheartedly accepted by Evan's friends."

"Isn't that what we all want?" Megan asked, sighing softly.

"Yeah, I suppose it is," Tucker said, tightening his arm around her waist so they were dancing close together to the romantic strains of "Close to You." He touched his face to hers. "I sure do like these slow numbers, dancing cheek to cheek and heart to heart with my favorite *cousin*," he whispered, brushing a soft kiss at her temple. "You know what?" he added, laughing softly. "This is what they mean when they say close as kissing kin, and I'm all for it!"

Chapter Six

"Megan, do you have a few minutes you can spare me?" Evan came through the door of Megan's office. "I need your help on something really important to me." There was an almost pleading look in his dark honey-colored eyes. "But I don't want to bother you if you're too busy."

"I'm not too busy at all, Evan. In fact I've finished all that was really vital for today. So tell me what I can help you with." She turned off the computer and watched as Evan walked over to her desk and plopped down in a nearby chair.

"Well, day after tomorrow is Linda's birthday. I want a really nice present for her, and I need your feminine input to choose what is exactly right.''

She smiled at him. ''You certainly can have it, Evan. I'm flattered that you're asking for my opinion. However, I will admit I have great taste in gifts, particularly when someone else is picking up the tab.'' She gave a light little laugh and then asked. ''Have you got something already in mind?''

He bobbed his head affirmatively. ''I've got three things picked out at Gordon's. If it's convenient I hoped you might be able to run over there late this afternoon with me and we'd choose which one together,'' he said, giving her an appealing smile.

''Ummm, Gordon's, that's an elegant jewelry store. It gives me a high just looking in their windows. I will *love* having an excuse to go inside.'' She sounded euphoric. ''How late are they open?''

''At least till five-thirty, and I think maybe till six.''

''Oh, that's good. I can leave the hospital a little early and meet you at Gordon's—say a quarter of five?''

''Don't you want me to pick you up?''

''No, I'm out of your way. Besides, Gordon's is in Garden Plaza Shopping Center and that's between the hospital and my house.''

"Okay then. I'll meet you there," he said as he leisurely pushed himself up out of his chair. "I sure appreciate this, Megan. You're my pal."

"Nope, I'm your redheaded cousin," she told him, laughing gaily.

An infectious grin spread across Evan's freckle-spattered face. "Well, I'll say this, Cousin. You sure came from the good-looking side of the family," he said as he left the records office.

The oblique shafts of late-afternoon sun shimmered across the plate-glass windows of the Garden Plaza shops. The entrance to Gordon's faced on a small courtyard with a gurgling fountain surrounded by a colorful array of summer flowers, namely white periwinkles, red impatiens, and yellow dwarf marigolds. Megan took a moment to admire the setting before she turned and entered the jewelry store.

Evan had gotten there ahead of her. He was standing in front of a display case waiting, and as she came to join him the jeweler spread a piece of black velvet on top of the case. He was a man of dignity, tall and poker-straight, probably in his early sixties. Megan watched him as he took three gold chain necklaces from the case and meticulously arranged each one on the velvet.

"Oh, Evan, these are all so pretty," she said,

leaning over, admiring them. "You couldn't go wrong with any one of them."

He looked pleased that she approved of his choices. "I like the way they all look, but which one do you feel would suit Linda the best?"

Megan continued to look closely and finger each of the chains, feeling the weight of them. "This is my least favorite," she said, indicating the middle one. "It has such tiny, fine links. Personally I like a bit heavier chain. One that seems substantial enough that you wouldn't worry about it breaking and causing you to lose the gold drop." She fingered the free-form gold nugget that hung on the delicate chain. "Now, this wider, serpentine chain is perfect." She picked it up and held it out in front of her. "Look how it glistens when the light catches it. It's beautiful. Actually, it could be worn effectively without the drop, when you wanted to."

"The lady is quite right about that, Dr. Kane. That particular type of chain is very versatile." The jeweler was quick to concur with Megan. "Too, you can select any of the drops you prefer to go with that chain. I'm sure you know that."

Megan looked at Evan questioningly. "In that case, Evan, shall we go with the serpentine chain?"

He nodded. "You've sold me," he agreed with

a chuckle. "Now, how about one of those thing-amabobs that hang on it?

"Well, we've looked at the nugget. It has an interesting shape to it, sort of modern free form." Megan was deliberately noncommittal. "Then there's this gold disk with a decorative filigree edge which is very pretty."

"Let me point out that we can personalize that by engraving it with the lady's monogram if you'd like," the jeweler intervened. "It's quite effective."

"That sounds nice. What do you think, Megan? Might that appeal to Linda?"

Megan looked at the disk, her lips pressed together in a concentrating line. "I—I think it would. I've seen monogrammed drops before and they're lovely." She hesitated, a tiny crease in her forehead marring her smooth features. "But it's not unusual, at least not nearly so as this." She leaned closer to the pieces displayed on the velvet in front of them, examining the intricate detail of a gold pendant in the graceful shape of a maple leaf. "Could you just slip this leaf on the serpentine chain we like, please?" she asked, bestowing a gracious smile on the patient man, who undoubtedly was praying that she and Evan would soon make up their minds so that he could conclude a sale by closing time. "I think that's perfectly beautiful!'' Megan exclaimed when the jeweler had it assembled. ''There's no girl alive who wouldn't be thrilled speechless to get this for her birthday.'' She shot a questioning glance toward Evan.

A smile broke from the corners of Evan's eyes, slashing lines in his lean cheeks. ''I wholeheartedly agree.'' He took his credit card out of his billfold and handed it to the pleased-looking older man.

When they left the store a few minutes later, Evan was carrying an elegantly gift-wrapped package, a look of complacency on his face. ''I couldn't have done this without you, Megan. A million thanks,'' he said, waving her off to her car.

''It was fun. I loved getting to help influence your choice,'' she said as they parted.

Megan didn't know what prompted her to do it, but as she backed out of her parking space she circled around the plaza, thus driving past where Evan was parked. She noticed that he hadn't opened his car door. In fact, it didn't look as if he intended to. Rather he was leaning against the side of his car with his head bent forward, and he appeared to be holding his nose between his fingers and his thumb.

Alarmed, for obviously Evan was in some distress, Megan quickly pulled her car into the nearest space, got out, and ran back to where he was.

"Evan, what's wrong? Are you sick? Are you hurt?" She hurled questions at him, staring at his colorless face anxiously.

He was breathing through his mouth, so he was slow to answer. "Got a nosebleed again," he said without looking up. "Darned nuisance. Can't risk bleeding on my car seats." He grunted disgustedly.

"Can I get something—wouldn't a cold, wet cloth help?"

"No, not much. Anyway, it'll stop in a minute or two."

"Are you sure? You honestly don't look like you feel at all well." She was really concerned about him. He looked so tired, as if he could barely stand. Too, she'd seen him wince and bend over more, as if he had some abdominal pain. "I think I should call Tucker."

"No!" he blurted. "Don't be ridiculous. A simple nosebleed is only a minor trauma. Everybody has one occasionally, and I assure you it's of little medical significance." He was more than a little irritated with her suggestion. He made that obvious by using his brand of doctor's phraseology to tell her to butt out.

"Okay, Evan. If it's only a simple nosebleed, as you say, then I'll get out of your way," she said evenly. "But the way I see it, you'd be doing yourself a favor to get a second opinion.'' Then feeling that anything else she might say or do would only upset him further, she walked slowly back to her car and drove away.

She felt a few qualms about driving off, but if Evan wasn't going to let her help him, what else could she do? And like he said, his nosebleed was not any medical emergency. Now in retrospect she began to feel foolish. Evan was a physician, for Pete's sake. Of course he didn't need a silly woman with a Florence Nightingale complex fluttering around telling him what he should do. She made a self-deprecating grimace and concentrated her attention now to her present problem of making it home through the heavy early-evening traffic.

The first thing she did when she got home was to change out of the tailored outfit she'd worn to work into something comfortable she could relax in. A few days ago at one of the end-of-summer sales she'd bought a pair of salmon-colored cotton slacks with a tunic-length overblouse. Megan had a sort of hangup about wearing something brand-new. She always wore it the first time at home to get accustomed to how it felt and the way it looked on her. She put her new outfit on now, reveling in its easy, relaxed fit and how comfortable it felt. A further spurt of pleasure ran though her when she looked at herself in the mirror and decided her new clothes looked even more attractive on her than she'd thought they did in the store.

Outside the sun was setting and the last rays of golden light filtered in through the west windows of the living room. Megan turned on a table lamp in the corner of the room near the fireplace before going into the kitchen to fix something for her dinner. Her attention was caught by the tiny red light flashing on her telephone answering machine. She quickly punched the button to hear the message.

"Hi Megan, it's me," Tucker's deep masculine voice informed her. "I'm hungry and I'm lonely, and I hope you are the same. Please stay right where you are and I'll be there at seven-thirty with a big pepperoni pizza with extra cheese and *no anchovies*." Tucker sounded so definite about the "no anchovies" that she chuckled out loud. In fact, his entire message amused her because such histrionics were unusual for him.

Still laughing about the hungry and lonely Tucker, she turned her head so she could see the time displayed on the microwave. "Seven twenty-three," she muttered under her breath. "Whew." She pushed a whistling sound through pursed lips, thinking that she hadn't gotten Tucker's message a minute too soon.

Immediately she yanked open the door to the

fridge to determine what she might have to make a salad. She let out a sigh of relief on finding leaf lettuce, one large tomato, a half of an avocado, and a partial bottle of Italian dressing. She quickly washed the lettuce and was in the process of shaking water off each leaf when Tucker arrived.

"I hope I didn't upset any of your plans, barging in without more notice than that message I left on your phone," he said, sounding somewhat apologetic as he marched toward the kitchen carrying the large pizza carton. "I did call you three times between about six and six-thirty. But you hadn't gotten home yet."

"I had some delays." She was deliberately nonchalant. She wasn't sure whether she should tell Tucker all about Evan yet or not. "Did Evan tell you he'd asked me to help him select a birthday gift for Linda?" she asked, starting now to put a salad together.

"Yeah, he said he was meeting you a little before five. It took you a long time, I guess."

"You know, it takes careful consideration. We wanted to make sure we settled on what would truly please Linda."

"And did you?"

"I'd say so. It's lovely and Linda should be thrilled," Megan explained as she cut the tomato into eight pieces, adding them to the bowl with the lettuce. She hesitated a second, then added, ''Something else occurred that I probably should tell you.''

''Hey, I bet I know what it is.'' He gave her a knowing look, and having set the pizza on the end of the counter, he now moved closer to Megan and stood watching her pull the thick green peeling from the avocado. ''Evan wanted your advice about an engagement ring, too, I'll bet.''

''Nope.'' She shook her head. ''He didn't mention anything but the necklace we decided on.'' She looked up at Tucker curiously. ''Do you really think Evan and Linda are that serious?''

''*He* is. Who knows about Linda. She's something of an enigma to me.'' Tucker thrust his hands into his pockets, a scowl erasing the good-natured look from his expression.

Megan thought she detected a hint of censure in his voice. She eyed him curiously. ''Don't you like Linda?''

''I like her all right; of course I do. Anyway, what's important is that Evan is truly in love with her. I just want her to be wholeheartedly committed to him, too.''

''My guess is that their feelings are mutual,'' Megan said, a reflective smile touching her lips.

''You've seen how Linda does everything she can to please Evan. That looks a lot like love to me. Wouldn't you agree?''

''I guess so. I don't really know.'' Tucker threw up his hands in resignation. ''How did we get into this sort of conversation anyhow? I came over here to further a romance of my own, not talk about my friend's love life.'' His eyes were caressing her face and a sensuous light smoldered in their depths.

Seeing the slumberous emotion glowing in Tucker's eyes made her tremble with happiness. Her heart sang and vibrated, feeling extraordinarily light and yet somehow enlarged, filling her whole chest cavity. He looked at her, she looked back, and for an instant something passed between them, some sense of curiosity, of trust, of . . . of perhaps love.

Chapter Seven

"I'll be gone for just a couple of minutes," Tucker said, turning on his heels and walking out of the kitchen. "When I come back I'll slice the pizza."

Megan nodded absently, as her attention was given to thoroughly shaking the contents of the bottle of salad dressing before dribbling it ribbon-like back and forth across the top of the salad she'd made.

True to his word, Tucker came back in a very short time. He immediately took up his task of cutting the large pizza into serving wedges with a pizza cutter. "Grab up the salad bowls and a couple of forks and follow me," he directed, a warm smile bringing an immediate softening to his features. And there was a self-satisfied glint in his eyes that caused Megan to wonder what he might be up to.

"Where are we going with it?" she asked, a note of curiosity in her voice. "I really thought we'd just eat right here in the kitchen."

"No way," he scoffed. "There's nothing romantic about this sleek black-and-white kitchen of yours. I just happen to have everything arranged in the living room for an intimate supper for us."

Tucker didn't give her a chance to aye or nay his plan, before leading her quickly through the arched doorway that led to the living room. Megan uttered an exclamation of surprise at what Tucker had done in those brief minutes he'd left her alone finishing the salad.

The ivory-colored mantel above the fireplace that usually was decorated with Megan's collection of brass candlesticks was bare. He had removed the candleholders and grouped them as to their various heights on the stone hearth, and now the many golden flames of the lighted candles flickered seductively in the darkened room. He also had placed two large pillows on the floor beside the low coffee table. "Now, isn't this nicer than the kitchen table?" he said, setting the pizza on the glass-topped table and taking the salad bowls out of Megan's hands and putting them there, too.

''Infinitely nicer,'' she agreed, smiling.

''Come sit beside me,'' he said, lowering himself onto one of the cushions and gently pulling Megan down to sit beside him. ''Don't you think eating by candlelight is going to be rather romantic?''

''Definitely romantic.'' Her voice was teasing and there was a mischievous glint in her eyes.

This light banter between them continued throughout their meal. After that they began speaking in gentle tones like two people do who were discovering they have a deep awareness of each other. They accompanied their words with soft touches and intimate smiles.

''Those candles are burning rather low,'' Megan announced with a sigh of regret. ''And much as I hate to disturb our romantic setting, I think I should blow them out and turn on some lamplight.''

''But you'd have to move away from me to do that,'' he moaned, looking devastated.

''Right. I can hardly blow them out from here,'' she said, laughing at his woebegone expression as she scrambled to her feet.

''Okay, but just don't turn on so many lamps

that you destroy the magic mood of this night.''

''Why don't you pick out the lamps to light while I put out the candles?''

''I can do that,'' he agreed, springing to his feet.

''Oh, and if you don't mind, pick up those two cushions and put them back on the sofa,'' she told him as she took down the brass candle snuffer off the mantel and bent down to snuff out the now-dwindling little flames. ''I think the sofa will be a more comfortable place for us to sit, don't you, Tucker?'' She stood up and turned to watch Tucker repositioning the big cushions. ''Unless you think that will diminish your night magic,'' she added, teasing him.

He gave her a provocative look. ''It could enhance it,'' he said, accompanying his words with a seductive smile. ''Shall I tell you how?''

She shook her head. ''Not until I tell you something about Evan that I think you really should hear.''

''Wow! Talk about shattering a romantic mood. Why on earth should we suddenly start talking about Evan when we could go on sharing our innermost thoughts with each other?''

''This will only take a minute, and I think it may be important.'' She walked over and sat down at one end of the divan, motioning to him to join her. ''You see, I learned something about Evan this afternoon and I really wanted to call you immediately. I would have, too, but when I suggested that to Evan he pooh-poohed it. Said it was nothing at all. In fact he got a little irritated with me and ran me off.''

Tucker stared at her, obviously totally confused by her outpouring of words. ''That's the most unclear set of statements I ever listened to,'' he said, frowning and shaking his head. ''Let's start this all over again at the beginning. What is it about Evan that you're trying to tell me?''

Megan sat forward, angling her shoulders so she could look directly at Tucker while she talked. ''Do you know if Evan has nosebleeds very often?'' she asked bluntly.

Tucker took his chin between his thumb and forefinger, frowning thoughtfully. ''I don't know how often, but now that you mention it, he did have one a month or so ago on the *ET*.''

''Well, he had another one today right after we left the jewelry store. And he spoke as if he had them frequently. Called them a pesky nuisance.'' She hesitated, a worried frown puckering her brow. ''I'd call this one more than a nuisance. It frightened me because Evan was bleeding a lot, and he couldn't stop it. He held his nose for what seemed like a long time to me, but the blood ran through his fingers. Then all at once he clutched his stomach with his other hand and bent over as if he had severe stomach pains. He wouldn't let me go get a wet cloth or anything to help. And when I said I wanted to call you, that was when he got angry. He used a lot of doctor talk, said a nosebleed was only a minor trauma and was of no medical significance. In no uncertain terms he told me to leave him to handle it and get on my way home.''

"That sure doesn't sound like Evan. He likes you, Megan. I'm surprised he'd push you aside like that . . . unless—'' Tucker stopped mid-sentence, a shadow of alarm touching his face.

"Unless what?'' she prodded him, her eyes intent on his.

"Unless he has good reason to suspect that his nosebleeds are indicative of something more serious.''

"Do you think that could be the case?''

"I don't want to think so, but Evan hasn't been up to par all summer,'' he said gravely. "We've all noticed that.'' He paused, shaking his head sadly. "And you mentioned he was experiencing abdominal discomfort. I don't like the sound of that. It could indicate an enlarged spleen.''

"Is that very serious?''

"It could be, coupled with anemia and the fact that Evan is so tired all the time. It's got to be looked into right away, that's for certain." He reached over and took Megan's hand, interlacing his fingers with hers. "You were right to tell me all of this, Megan. I'll find a way to talk to Evan about it tomorrow without fail. I'll convince him to have a complete blood workup and a thorough physical exam. In fact, with a little persuasion I think I can see that he gets it done before the end of the day tomorrow."

Megan heaved a troubled sigh. "Evan's liable to hate me for telling you all this."

"No he won't," Tucker assured her. "He'll understand that you were just concerned about him. Besides, he doesn't really have to know that you told me. I'll use a bit of subterfuge. I'll find a way to sort of sound him out about how he's been feeling lately. If I handle him right, he'll very likely tell me about the nosebleeds himself."

"Oh, if you could get him to do that, it would make it better all the way around."

He squeezed her hand. "I'll take care of it. Don't worry." He gave her a reassuring smile as he pulled her into the shelter of his arms. "Now I think it's high time we recapture that magic that we had before, don't you?" He looked at her, pushing the soft hair from her forehead and touching her eyelids and her lashes with his lips, then tracing the straight brows, the wide cheekbones, the short span of her nose, and the curve of her mouth. His gentle, physician's fingers touched her with wonder, as though he had never done this before. He bent to kiss her, his lips bruising in their need and intensity. The beautiful, heedless, all-enveloping waves of emotion drove everything else from Megan's mind. She put all her love into the soft yielding of her lips, and this magic night seemed to wrap itself around the two of them like warm velvet.

Chapter Eight

The remaining weeks of September passed, and the sad events of every day sifted down like the dry and faded autumn leaves. Evan had a series of blood tests and a biopsy of the bone marrow, and the diagnosis was chronic myeloid leukemia. When he revealed this to Linda, Tucker, and Megan, the four of them held each other like children warding off the dark, the terror that lay beyond their vision.

When Evan started on a program of chemotherapy, Tucker, Linda, and Megan became his support group. "The three of us are on Evan's team, and we're all going to do everything possible to help him beat this thing," Tucker declared vehemently.

"Isn't that right?" he asked. He looked at Linda as he said this, as if directing his question more to her than to Megan.

Linda lowered her eyes as if to escape Tucker's penetrating gaze. "You—you're a doctor, Tucker, so you would be able to do a lot of things for Evan. But what sort of help can I possibly offer him?" Her voice shook slightly and she pressed her lips together nervously.

"You can be there for him," Tucker commented bluntly.

Linda's moth-gray eyes brimmed with tears. "I've never been close to anyone with cancer before. I don't think I can bear the agony of standing around watching Evan slowly die."

Fierce anger blazed in Tucker's eyes. "Evan's not going to die!" he shouted, his voice vibrating with emotion. "Don't ever say that, and don't even think it for a second."

Linda let out an agonized sob, a crimson flush coloring her ivory skin. "For heaven's sake, Tucker, you don't need to yell at her," Megan said, immediately going over to Linda and putting her arms around the distraught woman's shoulders. "Can't you see how upset she is about this?"

"We're all upset about this," Tucker said tersely.

"Well, our getting angry with one another won't

help Evan. You should understand that neither Linda nor I know very much about leukemia. You could help us both by explaining what's happening to him. Please do that for us,'' she added, a pleading note in her soft voice.

''All right.'' Tucker's expression was tight with strain, but he began to explain everything to them in a patient, even consoling, tone of voice. ''Evan has chronic myelogenous leukemia. This is a malignant disease of the white cells in the circulating blood and bone marrow. It occurs most commonly in young men.'' He paused, crossing his arms across his chest. ''Now essentially that explains it. And, as we all know, Evan is already started on the standard treatment of chemotherapy, which will be followed by bone marrow transplantation. If we can find a compatible marrow donor, the transplant will give Evan his greatest chance for total recovery.''

Linda sighed and clasped her slender hands together. ''A bone marrow transplant—that sounds frightening, even gruesome.''

''Oh no.'' Tucker passed off her anxiety-filled words with a shrug. ''Not at all. Actually, it's a relatively simple procedure, both for the donor and recipient. The difficult part is to locate a compatible donor. You see, the unique characteristics of an individual's marrow are genetically inherited, the same way hair and eye color are. Which means that the ideal donors are tissue-matched family members, specifically a genetically matched sibling.''

''But Evan has no brothers or sisters,'' Linda replied in a small frightened voice. Anguish, stark and vivid, glittered in her eyes. ''Surely you both know that.''

Tucker nodded. ''We know that, Linda, but Evan still might have a chance of finding a family member who is a match. I thought I'd call his aunt in New Mexico. She's his mother's sister and the one who raised Evan after his parents died. I'm hoping that she possibly can tell me how to locate any other relatives of Evan's.''

Linda shook her head, her expression mutely wretched. ''But they still wouldn't be siblings. So it's hopeless, isn't it? There's really very little chance of finding a marrow donor for Evan, isn't there?''

''I'll find one,'' Tucker declared. ''You both wait and see.''

Megan sensed that Tucker's confident words and attitude were not only intended for their benefit but for his own as well. For she well knew that Tucker would move heaven and earth to save Evan's life.

The three of them had been huddled together talking in the hospital parking lot. They separated now, Linda and Megan to go home and Tucker to go in to the cancer treatment center of the hospital and pick up Evan to drive him home.

During the following weeks, Megan noticed that there was a difference to the slant of the morning light, and a noticeably sudden cooling of the nights. In the yards and parks the squirrels went at their work with a new urgency, the remaining fall asters finished blooming, and the leaves on the trees now came spinning down. Autumn had definitely arrived in Claysun.

Evan was midway through his chemotherapy. He felt extremely tired all the time now and his gaunt shoulders sagged with weariness. There were lots of days when he could hardly eat, so he'd dropped probably twelve to fifteen pounds. Along with losing weight he had also lost most of his handsome red hair. Whenever Linda, Megan, and Tucker prepared a dinner to tempt Evan's appetite and make a fun event of the four of them eating together like they always had before, at these times Evan often wore a baseball cap to cover his bare head. Linda had found a navy blue one that had DOCTOR DEAR lettered across the front of it. Megan and Tucker had ordered a crimson cap from a golf catalog and had OUR FAVORITE COUSIN in white letters emblazoned on it.

That evening when the meal was finished, Evan took off his cap and stretched out on the living room couch to rest and chat with Tucker while Linda and Megan were in the kitchen putting things in order and dishes in the dishwasher.

Coming back into the living room and seeing him with his head uncovered, Megan said, "Evan, you look every bit as handsome as Yul Brynner did in *The King and I*."

"Just as sexy, too," Linda chimed in, smiling at Evan and kissing two of her fingers, then touching them to the top of his head.

Megan was happy to see this gesture of affection from Linda and her caring expression. There was a depth to Linda's smile that had been missing too long. Maybe it meant that Linda was at last coming to terms with Evan's illness.

A short time later, Tucker and Megan left Evan's apartment. "I've got something I want to talk to you about," Tucker said, holding the car door open for Megan to slip into the passenger seat before he dashed around to the driver's side and slid in under the steering wheel. "I didn't want to bring this up in front of Evan, but I've talked on the phone to his aunt, and she made some curious, rather oblique statements that I think bear looking into.''

''Oh.'' There was a questioning inflection in Megan's voice. ''Do you think it could be something that will help us find a marrow donor for Evan?''

''I don't know. Maybe.'' Tucker's brows knitted in a puzzled frown. ''It was a strange conversation, and she sounded mysterious about what little she did say. I had the impression that she wanted to tell me something, but either was afraid to talk about it on the phone, or wouldn't because someone was there who might hear her.''

''And you believe she would tell you if you talked to her in person?''

''Yeah,'' he said with a decisive bob of his head. ''That's why you and I are going to fly to Roswell this weekend and talk to her.''

Tucker flipped the ignition switch and drove the car off into the murky night while Megan sat there staring at him for a full minute in stunned silence.

''Are you saying you want me to go with you for some reason?'' She looked every bit as confused as she sounded. Because, for the life of her, she couldn't imagine why Tucker would want her to tag along to a meeting with Evan's aunt.

''You could be a real help, Megan. You know how women are. They usually will talk more freely to another woman than to a man." He sidled a look at her, flashing one of his charm-laden smiles. "It will make it a fun trip if you're with me. I was looking forward to your sitting beside me while a grateful patient of mine flies us in his Beechcraft Bonanza out to Roswell next Saturday morning. We'll have lunch there, then an hour or so visit with Evan's aunt and uncle, and then head back to Claysun late that afternoon. How does that sound to you?"

"Like a very full and interesting day, I'd say. But—" Megan's face clouded with uneasiness.

"But what?" Tucker prodded her to finish her sentence.

"But I've never flown in a small plane before," she muttered, chewing the corner of her lip nervously. "Tell me about this grateful patient of yours. Is he really an experienced pilot?"

"Yes, he sure is." He took his right hand off the steering wheel and reached over to pat her arm reassuringly. "Joe Sherrill is his name. He was in the Air Force, had over a thousand hours of flight time. Now he and his brother are in the oil business together. They have production in Kansas, Oklahoma, Texas, and New Mexico. Joe flies over this area all the time, knows it like the back of his hand. There's nothing to worry about."

"I suppose not," she said, but there wasn't much conviction in her subdued tone of voice.

"Then you'll go with me Saturday?"

"I will if it's a bright clear day and all the conditions are right for a safe flight." Her uncertainty caused her voice to waver.

"Hey, don't you worry. I promise we won't fly unless all systems are go. Deal?"

"Deal," she answered, mustering up an agreeing smile.

"And you mustn't forget, Megan, that the powers that be have ordained me to be responsible for your safety at all times."

"They have?" She raised her eyebrows, looking skeptical. "When did all this happen, and what do you mean 'the powers that be'?"

"Well, back when this area of the Southwest was Indian Territory, the Indians believed that when two people's paths cross—as ours did that fateful afternoon in the hospital parking lot, when I was able to get you out of harm's way—they take that as a sign from the Great Spirit."

"A sign of what?" she asked, bewildered by Tucker's reference to old Indian lore.

"That from that particular moment I was destined to be your protector and always see after your safety."

"How nice for me," she said, a soft smile moving across her lips. "And I thought the age of chivalry was dead."

"Nope. Not as long as a few old Indians and I are around, it's not," he replied, smiling at her with beautiful candor. "And I'll stay around a long time, too, if you like." He covered her hand with his as he spoke and gave her a smile to match the warmth of his hand.

It felt good having her narrow hand secured beneath his firm, square one. She nodded her head. "I like," she said.

Chapter Nine

It was not too long after sunrise when Megan climbed out of bed on Saturday. She dressed carefully but quickly, for Tucker was to pick her up in less than an hour. The two of them were scheduled to meet Joe Sherrill at the airport, ready for takeoff by eight. Tucker had promised to bring along her favorite apricot Danish rolls and a large thermos of coffee so they could have breakfast together on the plane. He had really wanted her to make this trip with him—he'd made that abundantly clear—and now he certainly was trying to think of everything he could to make it enjoyable for her. She sensed this was partly because he knew she really wasn't too keen about flying in a small plane. She smiled inwardly, remembering the Indian legend Tucker had recounted to her. Since fate had destined Tucker to be her protector, was she not safe from all harm?

Once Megan looked out her windows and saw that it was going to be a clear and perfect day, she could only feel good about everything. After all, she'd always thought October was the most beautiful month of the year here in Claysun. This particular autumn morning was touched with gold, as shafts of sunlight cut through the misty dawn. A spider's web that stretched between two of the limbs of an elm tree looked like a piece of silk strung with dew-pearls that sparkled under the beams of the sun.

When Tucker and Megan arrived at the airport, Tucker parked his car by the fence next to the hangar where Joe kept his plane. ''We got here in plenty of time,'' he told Megan as the two of them were walking toward the hangar. ''I see ol' Joe is still busy checking out the plane.'' He directed Megan's attention toward a medium-size man with curly black hair wearing jeans and a T-shirt who was circling the Beechcraft, apparently inspecting the plane's surface.

''She looks good to me; how does she look to you?'' Tucker asked as he and Megan came up alongside the plane.

"A-okay," Joe replied, saluting them by making an affirmative okay circle with his thumb and middle finger, then bestowing a grin of welcome to Megan. "I've checked the engine, fuel, oil, prop, and landing gear. All systems are go."

"Good, 'cause I think Megan here can use some assurance that this plane of yours can get us to Roswell and back."

"Hey, this little lady is fit and fair and sturdy as they come," Joe said, patting the side of the fuselage. "Yet like any lady she demands constant attention. So I'm careful to give her my tender loving care, and she never lets me down. I promise you she'll take us where we want to go and bring us back safe and sound." He emphasized his words with a confident bob of his head followed by a smile that mellowed the hard, strong lines of his suntanned face.

"I know that," Megan said. "And I'm really not worried. Tucker just likes to make a big thing out of the fact that the most I know about flying is checking my luggage and collecting my boarding pass."

Joe laughed. "Well now, we'll see that you know more than that before this day is over. Won't we, Tucker?" Joe commented as he walked to the door of the plane and opened it. "Come on. Let's get started. Megan, you ride in the cockpit with me. I fly from the left seat so I'll crawl in first. Tucker will sit behind you.''

Megan and Tucker quickly complied with Joe's seating orders. Once inside the plane, however, Megan's earlier apprehension at the thought of flying in a small aircraft returned. Not wanting to risk any further comments from Tucker, she tried to force herself to relax. To this end, the comfortable contours of the leather upholstered seat helped, for it fit smoothly to her back, giving her support. Her eyes were drawn to the panel in front of her, full of complicated instruments and switches, some fifteen or twenty of them grouped with the engine controls. Although she should have found this scientific instrumentation reassuring, somehow the sight was awesome, and did little to relieve her inner tensions.

Glancing up, she discovered the nicest feature of the plane: the curved, formed plastic windshield that appeared to open up the entire sky to her. Perhaps if she concentrated on the serene blue of the heavens and the clear light of the morning sun, she would be able to enjoy the flight that lay ahead. Realizing that she was actually holding her breath, she let it out quietly, hoping Joe and Tucker hadn't noticed this additional sign of her anxieties.

''Time to fasten up,'' Joe ordered, snapping the metal buckles on his own seat belt. As soon as

Tucker and Megan did the same, Joe called the Claysun tower for clearance. "Bonanza, November 4–5–0 Juliet Sierra ready to go on one eight."

Seconds later a voice rasped from the speaker overhead. "Bonanza, November 4–5–0 Juliet Sierra cleared for takeoff."

From that moment on Megan watched in fascination as Joe advanced the throttle levers and the engine crescendoed until the sound was like a scream of a banshee. As the plane accelerated down the runway, Megan could feel the force of a dozen invisible hands pressing her body into the contours of her seat. She saw Joe glance at the heading indicator as the plane climbed to get clear of the airspace around the airport.

"What are we doing now?" she asked, wanting to understand something of what was going on.

"We're reaching our desired heading," he explained. "After we're on course I'll engage the autopilot." His manner was offhand, and very shortly he moved his hand on the switch. The wings jerked quickly and Megan caught her breath in excited interest. Joe's eyes seemed to be intently searching every gauge. She watched his fingers gliding deftly to adjust the knobs and press switches. When all was apparently satisfactory, he looked out at the sky with a satisfied smile and eyes that sparkled with achievement.

Observing him, Megan had the feeling that, for a few minutes at least, Tucker's friend had escaped into another world. A world where only he and his plane existed. She smiled inwardly at the thought, and for the first time since she'd climbed aboard the Bonanza she relaxed. Then turning her head she looked over her shoulder at Tucker and said, "You were right about this. You said it was going to be a fun trip."

"Then I guess you're beginning to like Joe's little plane," Tucker said, putting his hand on her shoulder and leaning around the back of her seat to talk to her.

"What's not to like? Didn't one of you tell me that the Beechcraft Bonanza is the finest single-engine complex airplane in the world today?"

"If he didn't, I will," Joe interjected. "That's not just hype either. It's a fact."

"I believe it. You've both convinced me," she added with a light laugh. "But now there's some of the airplane business I'm curious about."

"What's that?"

An inquisitive frown narrowed her eyes. "It's that jargon you pilots use to identify yourself. But what in the world does November and that Juliet Sierra stuff have to do with it?"

"Simple. Those words stand for the letters N, J, and S, actually. We use words for each letter in the alphabet so that we can be sure we're understood. For example, A is Alpha, B is Bravo, C is Charlie, and so on. You follow me so far?''

''Yeah.'' She nodded. ''But explain why you start out with November.'' Her eyebrows raised inquiringly.

''Well.'' Joe paused and folded his hands together comfortably. ''N is the international designation for all United States registered aircraft. That's official. So Bonanza N identifies my type of plane and the fact that it's a United States aircraft. Now, the 4–5–0 and the J S were my choice. I picked these numbers and letters to identify me and what I do.'' He inclined his head toward her and there was a twinkle of humor in his eyes. ''A bit of my ego showing, you might say.''

''Oh, there's nothing wrong with a pilot using his own initials. But only another 'fly boy' would figure out that Juliet Sierra in the final analysis stood for Joe Sherrill.'' She teased him with a wry chuckle as she added, ''So you're ego really doesn't show at all.''

''I think your female passenger is ribbing you, Joe,'' Tucker said.

Megan shook her head. ''No, not really,'' she countered quickly. ''This whole business is totally new to me. It all fascinates me. I want to hear more.''

"Me, too." Tucker stuck his head into the space between Megan's and Joe's seat. "You said you chose something that signified the work you do. What's that?"

"That's my numbers 4–5–0. That's the clever bit," he said, sounding cocky.

"How so? Tell us about it."

"Thought you'd never ask." He chuckled. "It took me a while to come up with something that would relate to our business. Since the Bonanza is our company plane, I really wanted to tie it in if I could figure a way. I finally came up with the right numbers—4–5–0. Can you guess why they are significant?"

Tucker shook his head. "Haven't got a clue."

"It's basic. My brother's and my little company has oil production in four of the fifty states. So at least those numbers mean something to the two of us."

"And they mean Kansas, Texas, Oklahoma, and New Mexico to me."

Joe beamed with pleasure at her words. "You're a sharp gal, Megan. You guessed that one exactly right."

Tucker looked amused. "She's a quick study all right. Has a good memory for details, too."

Megan gave him an arch look. "That's a back-handed compliment if I ever heard one. Tucker is making sure, Joe, that you know it wasn't a guess. See, he told me that you knew the area between Claysun and Roswell like the back of your hand because you flew over it all the time in your business.''

''Well, I'd say having a good head for details makes you as smart as a tree full of owls,'' Joe joked.

''And I'd say it's time to cut out this smart talk and enjoy a Danish and this thermos of coffee I brought,'' Tucker said with a jovial laugh. ''I don't know about you two, but I haven't had any breakfast yet and I'm hungry. . . .''

Chapter Ten

The flight to New Mexico was so smooth and level that the small plane felt almost motionless, as if it were simply suspended in the blue morning sky. They landed at the airport at Roswell shortly before noon. Joe took off again to be about his business, promising Tucker and Megan that he'd be there to pick them up at three-thirty that afternoon for the trip back to Claysun. Tucker had reserved a rental car for them, and the man at the car agency recommended a good restaurant where they could go for lunch before their scheduled visit with Evan's aunt and uncle.

The restaurant had a colorful southwestern decor, and the tantalizing odors of spicy peppers and pungent herbs added authentic Mexican flavor. "This place looks and smells intriguing," Megan commented in a pleased tone as they sat down at a table for two at one side of the room.

"Right. And the food must be good, too. I didn't see but a couple of empty tables." Tucker opened the menu. "I bet they serve first-rate tacos and enchiladas."

Megan scanned the menu quickly. "I'm going to have the chicken chimichangas with sour cream, guacamole, and cheddar cheese."

"I won't argue with that. Make it two," Tucker addressed the attractive Hispanic waitress who stood, pad in hand, ready to take their order.

"What time are we to meet Evan's aunt and uncle?" Megan asked, dipping a crisp taco chip into some salsa to munch on while they waited for their lunch to be served.

"Between one and one-thirty," he mumbled as he followed her lead with the chips and hot sauce. "Gives us plenty of time to enjoy our lunch."

"Do you know how to find their house, do you think?"

"Shouldn't be any problem. His aunt gave me directions to get from the airport to their place, and it happens that this restaurant is on the main avenue we're to follow till we come to a major intersection that shouldn't be but about another couple of miles from here. I'll check that out with our waitress before we leave.''

''I'm sort of leery about this, Tucker.'' She fingered the sides of her water glass absently. ''You know Evan's aunt and uncle, but I'm a total stranger. They may not talk freely to you with me there.''

Tucker shrugged. ''They don't know me either, really. I only met them one time and that was when Evan and I graduated from med school.''

''I know. But you're Evan's friend and his colleague and they know how much you want to help him. I want something good to come out of this for Evan. I sure don't want to hamper that in any way.'' Her earnest eyes sought his.

''You won't, believe me.'' He inclined his head toward her, a tender smile warming his eyes. ''I've got a good gut feeling about this. You and Evan's Aunt Dorcas are going to hit it off just great. She'll probably talk up a storm with you.''

''Good, I hope so. You did say, though, that she acted a little strange on the phone with you. Wouldn't explain anything about why she wanted to see you.''

''I know. When you meet her you'll see what a mild, sweet little lady she is. Right now, however, she's terribly anxious and emotional about Evan, of course.'' He hesitated, frowning thoughtfully.

"My guess is that Dorcas needs to talk about Evan with you and me because we see him every day, and know about his treatment and what's going on with him. She's looking for an emotional crutch to lean on, I think."

"Aren't we all?" Megan said with a sigh.

Tucker had been right about Dorcas and Jim Naylor's house. They had no difficulty at all in locating it. It was the usual ranch style of most of the houses in the same neighborhood. However, instead of being dark brick and redwood as many of the homes were, the Naylor house was a very light tan brick with sienna brown trim and a decorative stained wood front door.

When Tucker pressed the doorbell it chimed way inside, two notes echoing oddly like some strange birdcall. There was only a momentary delay before the door opened and a little round woman stood there, cozy as an armchair upholstered in a navy and white print dress.

"Oh, you're here!" she exclaimed, a smile creasing her pleasant face. "Come in, come in quickly. Jim wants a chance to see you and hear about Evan before he has to do some work. Wouldn't you know he'd get two repair calls just before you got here. Appliance repairs, that's his business, you know." She spoke in a rapid burst of words as she led Megan and Tucker into a light-oak paneled family room, comfortably furnished in easy-to-live-with colors, carefully blended to capture the essence of springtime no matter what the weather outside. The lack of draperies was not obvious in the room, as it seemed quite natural to have the sunlight filter through the foliage beyond the windows that looked out onto a patio and fill the room with natural light.

Dorcas introduced Megan to her husband and as soon as Megan explained that she worked at the same hospital with Evan and Tucker and that they were all friends, she walked over and sat down in a deep-cushioned lounge chair, leaving the divan and a club chair next to it for the Naylors and Tucker. With a gracious wifely gesture, Evan's aunt took her place at the far end of the sofa and laid her hands open-palmed in her lap, relinquishing all conversation to her husband. Jim began at once to question Tucker about Evan's condition, wanting a detailed account of the treatment Evan was undergoing and asking for Tucker's evaluation of the medical possibilities of remission of the leukemia for him.

Megan studied the older man as the two of them talked. Jim Naylor seemed to be a stolid sort of man, calm, slow spoken, and methodical. He was a medium-size man with curly dark hair liberally mingled with gray. Megan guessed his age at fifty-five to sixty.

Dorcas sat very still, listening closely to all that was being said. She made no attempt to ask any questions of her own or even to take part in the men's conversation. Megan glanced at her, sensing that Evan's aunt had something she wanted to say, but wasn't ready just yet to speak up. *She's waiting for something to happen,* Megan thought. Then for no explainable reason it suddenly occurred to Megan that this quiet, mild-mannered little woman was waiting for her husband to leave before she talked to Tucker about Evan.

"So far, Evan's been able to tolerate his treatment fairly well," Tucker was saying. "But it's still too soon to evaluate the benefits he may have gained from chemotherapy." He hesitated, clearing his throat as he looked from Jim to Dorcas. "I'm sure you both realize that the only real hope is that somehow we can find a compatible bone marrow donor for him."

At this, Dorcas's head drooped sadly, her lids sank slowly over her eyes, and two crystal tears slid down her grave face.

"We were both tested and we're not a match." Jim's breath rasped harshly in his throat, and his expression was bleak.

"I know that." Tucker nodded glumly. "The

sad thing is that the only real chance of finding a match is from a sibling.''

''We were told that.'' Jim looked morose for a long moment before getting slowly to his feet. ''I appreciate your coming and telling us about Evan. Thank you, Tucker.'' He took Tucker's hand and shook it warmly. ''I have to go do my work now,'' he said. ''I'm sorry to have to leave, but in the appliance repair business you work six days a week.'' He turned toward Megan. ''It's nice to meet good friends of Evan's. You do everything you can for him, won't you?'' Then he looked toward his wife. ''I'll try to get home by five o'clock, Dor,'' he told her as he hurried out of the room.

As soon as he was gone, Dorcas gave a pleasant hostess-like smile to her guests. ''I hope you like homemade butterscotch cookies. They're Evan's favorite and I baked a batch this morning for you to take back to him. I thought we could have our visit over a cup of coffee and a cookie. Would you like that?''

''How nice. Of course we would,'' Megan said quickly, giving Tucker a silencing look so he wouldn't tell Evan's aunt that they'd just finished eating lunch and couldn't eat or drink another thing. ''Let me help you.''

''No need, my dear. I have it all ready in the

kitchen. It'll just take me a minute to bring it in.'' She bounced up off the divan and bustled out of the room.

Megan moved from her chair to the end of the sofa where Dorcas had been sitting, leaving the spot closer to Tucker for Dorcas to take when she returned. ''I think she's really anxious to talk to you about Evan.'' She spoke in a stage whisper, not wanting to risk Dorcas overhearing her.

Tucker shrugged, looking skeptical. ''Well, we'll see. But there sure hasn't been a peep out of her about him so far.''

''I think that's because she was waiting for her husband to leave.''

''Really?'' Tucker angled his head questioningly. ''You mean because he was going out right away, she wanted him to have every chance to ask questions and learn what he wanted to know about Evan's prognosis?''

''That might be part of it, but I don't think it's all of it.'' She hesitated, a frown puckering her brow. ''I'm only guessing, you understand. But the way she sat here, patiently and quietly biding her time, made me think that whatever she has to say to you she doesn't want to say in front of her husband.''

He formed his hands into a pyramid and rested his chin on the square fingers, a thoughtful expression on his face. "You might be right about that. It could explain why she wouldn't tell me anything on the phone, too, if Jim was around the house when we were talking. Seems odd, but it sure is a possibility."

They stopped talking then as they could hear Dorcas returning. As she came through the doorway Tucker jumped to his feet and took the loaded tray she was carrying from her. He indicated that she should take the seat on the sofa her husband had vacated, and as soon as she was settled he set the tray on the coffee table in front of her. Looking pleased by his gentlemanly attentions, Dorcas served their coffee and passed around a plate of her homemade cookies with a gracious manner.

"I sure know why these are Evan's favorites," Megan said as soon as she'd tasted one. "They're yummy."

"You can say that again," Tucker echoed Megan's compliment.

Dorcas smiled, causing two dimples to appear as if loving fingers had squeezed her cheeks. "Growing up, Evan always liked my cookies and a glass of milk at bedtime." She gave a soft little sigh and added, "I bet he could use a little fattening up with a bedtime snack these days. That's why I have a big tin of butterscotch cookies fixed for you to take back to him."

"Oh, that will be a great treat for him. He'll love it," Megan said enthusiastically. She sensed how important it was to Dorcas to do something caring and motherly for Evan and she wanted to make her feel good about this.

"I want us to talk about Evan now," Dorcas said, placing her coffee cup down gingerly in its saucer. "Evan has got to beat this cancer, and there's just the slightest chance that I can help you get the right bone marrow transplant that he must have to save his life."

Tucker leaned forward in his chair, eyeing Evan's aunt curiously. "Exactly what do you mean by right?" he asked.

"I mean a match, of course." Her face was pink with eagerness.

He continued to stare at her intently. "But you know the only chance for a true match is from a sibling."

She nodded, but didn't speak.

"And Evan doesn't have any brothers or sisters," Megan murmured glumly.

"Yes he does!" There was an almost defiant ring to her voice. "He has a sister."

Tucker's body jerked to attention. "Evan has a sister?" He sounded disbelieving. "That's impossible. He never spoke of any sister. He never talked of anyone but just his parents. How could

he have a sister and never talk about her—unless—''
He paused, a shocked expression on his face. ''He
doesn't even know about her, does he?''

Dorcas's heightened color subsided. ''None of
us know much of anything about her.''

''What do you mean? You know she exists;
that's what counts. So who is she? Where is she?
I've got to contact her right away.'' Tucker hurled
questions at her, running his words together in his
eagerness.

Evan's aunt held her hands up defensively.
''Please. Give me a chance to explain.''

''Yes, Tucker. Knock it off with the questions,''
Megan cautioned him with a warning look. ''Let
Dorcas tell us about all this in her own way.''

His face tightened in impatience. ''Okay, sure,''
he muttered as he shifted in his chair and crossed
his legs.

Megan inched a bit closer to Dorcas and put her
hand on the older woman's arm, patting her gently.
''Tucker didn't mean to come on so strong, but
you can't blame him for getting excited over your
surprising news. We all want a miracle for Evan
and you may be able to give us one.''

''I'm hoping so, too. Only there's such a few
things for us to go on.'' Her faint smile held a
touch of sadness. ''You know, Evan was only six
years old when we took him after the tornado.''

She hesitated a second, absently tucking a loose strand of gray hair into place. "That was early in June, and my sister, Arlene, Evan's mother, was pregnant, expecting the baby sometime in August. The tornado struck late that afternoon. Evan's dad was killed when it happened, and by the time they got Arlene to a hospital there was little hope of saving her and even less chance, they thought, for her baby. Arlene did die while they were performing the cesarean," Evan's aunt said tonelessly, before blowing a soft sigh through her narrow lips.

"But the baby was all right, wasn't she?" Megan questioned anxiously.

"She was very tiny. Weighed barely three pounds, they told me." Dorcas shook her head as she said this. "And they talked about respiratory distress."

"That often happens in a premature birth," Tucker said. "A little preemie doesn't always breathe spontaneously. But they have specialized equipment and skilled staff ready for resuscitation. Was this a fairly big hospital?"

"It was the hospital where you and Evan are now, St. Mark's. The ambulance brought Arlene to Claysun because it was the closest city that wasn't in the path of the tornado."

Tucker registered surprise. "I didn't know that. I only knew that Evan was born in a small town in Kansas. I just never thought of it being in the radius of Claysun. Good thing though, because even twenty-five or so years ago St. Mark's would have had the finest medical equipment and a highly competent staff. Evan's newly born sister was in good hands, I'd say. I bet they put her on a respirator and apnea monitor immediately, didn't they?''

''I suppose so. When Jim and I saw her she was in an incubator with wires and tubes connected to her everywhere. And she was so tiny. No bigger than a doll. It was frightening, and I could hardly look at her because they had already told us that there was very little chance that she would live.''

''The doctor told you that the first time you saw her?'' Tucker asked.

Dorcas nodded. ''Yes, both the doctor who had delivered her and the pediatrician they had called in to take care of her. He was kind—took time to explain it all carefully to us. He said an infant that is born two months premature often has this respiratory distress syndrome. He called it by another name, though, that I've forgotten now.''

''Hyaline membrane disease,'' Tucker prompted her.

''Yes, that sounds like it, as I remember.''

A thoughtful frown creased Megan's brow.

''That's what the Kennedy baby died with, isn't it, Tucker?''

''Yes,'' he answered her tersely. ''But let's hear what the pediatrician told Dorcas.'' He shot Megan an oblique look of reprimand.

''He wanted us to realize that Arlene's baby had two strikes against her, and that chances were slim that she could make it.''

''But she did!'' Megan's voice spiraled in excitement. ''Evan's little sister is alive, and she can help him. Oh, Tucker, isn't that wonderful?''

At Megan's outburst of words, an expression of anguish darkened Dorcas's face. ''No, no,'' she cried. ''I don't know that. I-I don't actually know that she's alive. I never even knew for certain that she didn't die there in the hospital.''

Tucker stared at Evan's aunt, a look of shocked disbelief darkening his eyes. ''That's impossible! How on earth could you not know a thing like that?''

The older woman twisted her hands together nervously. ''When we left the hospital that day, that was the last I knew. We were never told anything about what happened to Arlene's baby after that.'' Dorcas looked down at her hands and pressed them into her lap so they were partially hidden in the folds of her skirt. ''You have to understand that we had to leave Claysun with Evan and drive back to Roswell. Jim had to get back to his business, and the telephone company where I worked had allowed me only three days off. It was especially important, now that we had Evan to care for, that I didn't do anything that might jeopardize my job.'' She spoke with quiet, but desperate, firmness. ''Evan was going to be our son now. Jim and I were determined to provide everything we possibly could for him.'' She lifted her chin as she said this, meeting Tucker's gaze straight on.

''And I'm sure you did,'' Megan said.

Dorcas made an attempt to smile. ''We did what we felt was best at the time, which explains why Evan didn't ever know he had a sister. Jim believed it would be a big mistake to tell Evan right away. I agreed, because here he was, a sad little boy who had just lost his mother and his father. That was trauma enough for any child. And besides, how can you make a six-year-old boy understand that he had a sister who was born too soon and too small to be able to live?'' Her voice faltered, and Megan could see that Dorcas was fighting back tears.

After a long pause during which Dorcas struggled for self-control, she continued. ''I really intended to tell Evan when he grew older, but before that time came Jim admitted to me what he had done. I knew then that I could never tell Evan at all. In fact, I hoped I never would have to tell anyone.''

Dorcas's anguish was obvious and drew Megan's sympathy. ''I know this is hard for you to talk about,'' Megan told her. ''But we need to know anything that might enable us to help Evan. So, do you feel you could explain whatever it is that your husband did?'' Megan asked gently.

Dorcas looked from Megan to Tucker, an agonized expression drawing her brows together. ''I know I must tell you. But please, before you pass judgment on Jim, remember that we're a family with only a modest income. Jim was forced to make a realistic and reasonable decision. He signed a waiver giving up any rights we would have to Arlene's child.''

''That would explain why they didn't notify you about what happened to her,'' Tucker said, rubbing his hand across his forehead thoughtfully.

Megan looked puzzled. ''But surely they'd have notified Dorcas and Jim if the baby had died. After all, even if they couldn't assume financial responsibility for her, they were her aunt and uncle.'' Suddenly she sucked in her breath, her eyes flaring wide with excitement. ''Oh my golly, Tucker. You know what this means? Evan's sister didn't die. She's alive. She must be alive. That's the reason

Dorcas and Jim never heard anything more about her. If she had died in the hospital they would have had to notify the next of kin. But the doctors and nurses were able to save her, and then because Jim had signed whatever the agreement was, why, then some other family took her. Don't you see, that has to be what happened!'' This torrent of words poured from Megan's mouth, and she only stopped to catch her breath, before turning to Tucker. ''You do think I'm right, don't you?''

''I sure as anything am going to find out.'' The hard, strong lines of Tucker's face mirrored the determination in his voice. He got to his feet as he said this and came over to the sofa, extending his hand to Dorcas. ''You can count on us, I promise you that.'' There was a reassuring note in his voice and in the confident way he held his head and shoulders. ''As soon as we get back to Claysun, Megan will search through the hospital records concerning Arlene Kane and her baby. The first thing I'll do is enlist the help of a private investigator. We'll talk to any doctors and nurses we can find who were working at St. Mark's at the time Evan's sister was born. I can guarantee that we'll learn what happened to her back then and where she is right now. And when we find her, we'll have our bone marrow donor for Evan. Thanks to you.''

Dorcas smiled with white lips, her small square hand gripping Tucker's hand so tensely that her knuckles were whitening as well. Her face was pale, her wrinkled throat working convulsively. She swallowed once and said, ''I pray I didn't wait too long. We must not fail Evan. . . .''

Chapter Eleven

Soon after that Tucker mentioned that it was
time for him and Megan to leave. Megan was relieved, because she knew it would be easier on
Dorcas to have them gone before her husband returned. In the past hour emotions had run high for
all of them. Visible signs of stress were evident on
Dorcas's grave face. She would surely welcome
time to compose herself before she faced her husband and revealed that she'd told Evan's friends
about his sister.

They left, driving along the streets of Dorcas's
neighborhood in a thoughtful sort of silence. No
one was outside in the yards as they passed and
all seemed quiet around them, no signs of activity

126

anywhere. Mid-afternoon in New Mexico obviously was siesta time, Megan thought, but she didn't voice this speculation to Tucker. Instead, she gazed out the car window, observing how the October sunlight spread a lacy pattern across the browning grass and admiring the blooming chrysanthemums in their muted shades of autumn.

A few minutes later they had driven beyond the residential area and were back on the main thoroughfare. Tucker drew the car to a halt at a stoplight and waited for the light to change from red to green.

"Megan," Tucker spoke her name, breaking into her idle reverie.

She turned her head to look at him and he leaned over and kissed her. "Why did you do that?" she asked, totally surprised by his unexpected behavior.

"I just felt like it." He grinned, driving ahead as the light changed. "Besides, you seemed so quiet and far away, and I wanted to do something to get your attention."

"Well, you got it all right." She grinned back at him. "Does that tactic always work on the women you've tried it on?"

"I don't know yet, I'll be glad to do it again and you can tell me."

She started to quip that he was quite the smooth

talker, but then she thought better of it. After all, she liked what he'd said. And because she was so completely enamored of Tucker, she wanted to believe that he was beginning to think of her as more than just a member of his foursome of close friends, the ''cousin'' that he felt destined to keep out of harm's way. On the other hand, she'd better not let herself make anything much out of a few romantic words and kisses, or she could end up a fool with a broken heart.

''Hey! I thought you said I had your attention. If I did I sure wasn't able to keep it very long,'' Tucker said, feigning a look of dejection.

''You do have it. I just had something to think about for a minute.'' She slanted her eyes up at him. ''Sorry,'' she murmured contritely.

''Well, whatever it was, stop thinking about it. It couldn't have been too pleasant. You looked as if it had just rained on your parade.''

She shrugged. ''I'll put up my umbrella and march on,'' she countered glibly. ''And now tell me, were you as surprised as I was about Evan having a sister?''

''Astounded is more like it.''

''Do you really think we have a prayer of finding her?'' she asked, switching her position and angling her back into a corner of the seat so she could study Tucker's profile as they talked and he drove.

''I'd say there's a fifty-fifty chance at least.'' He took one hand off the steering wheel and flexed his fingers. ''Since it all happened at St. Mark's, we could get lucky.'' He made a fist and held it up for a moment before placing his hand back on the wheel.

''Are you going to tell Evan about her?''

Tucker shook his head. ''No way!'' he said emphatically. ''We don't dare get his hopes up until we can be sure she's alive, and we've got concrete evidence to go on to locate her.''

Megan's expression was troubled. ''How can we keep him from finding out when we're going through hospital records and talking to people at St. Mark's who were around when it all happened? Isn't he bound to get wind of it?'' Her voice mirrored her anxieties.

''We'll have to be extremely cautious, that's all. And the doctors and nurses who we talk to will understand why we have to keep it from Evan right now, at least. We all know that it's far too emotional a situation for Evan to deal with at the moment.'' He nodded his head and shot her a reassuring look. ''It'll be okay, trust me.''

They didn't talk further because they had arrived back at the airport. They had only time enough for Tucker to turn in their rental car, and the two of them to hightail it to where they were to meet Joe for the flight back to Claysun.

Tucker had promised to treat them all to dinner that night. They arrived in Claysun a little after seven and since both Joe and Tucker had left cars parked near the hangar where Joe kept his plane, Tucker led the way to the restaurant and Joe trailed him in his car. Tucker told Megan he was taking them to The Stonehurst, a recently opened restaurant located in a converted stone mill about six miles east of Claysun on the old Post Road. Megan had heard about the place, but she hadn't been there. "I've been told the food is great, and that old grist mill is a unique setting. I can't wait to see it," she told Tucker.

"I hoped you'd like the idea," he said. "And I thought it would be an interesting way to pay Joe back for flying us around the country today."

When they drove up to the gray stone mill, warm yellow light shone from behind small windows and spilled from the crooked doorway. The sign over the door swung and creaked a bit in the light night breeze. There were a number of cars parked outside. Tucker inserted his neatly into a space next to a minivan, and Joe pulled in beside him.

The interior was interesting and unusual with its stone walls and low ceilings, and it smelled like a herb garden after a rain shower, having the pleasing odors of parsley, sage, savory, thyme, rosemary, basil, and fresh-cut mint. It was not a large room and most of the tables were already occupied. But a young man approached them with a smile that etched lines down his thin brown cheeks and creased his eyes. ''Good evening,'' he said, and immediately led them to what looked to be the best table in the room, set in a windowed alcove.

As soon as they were seated, the waiter explained that there were no menus at The Stonehurst and the only choice for each of them to make was their entrée. ''We serve club or sirloin steak, prime rib, or rack of lamb.''

Megan and Joe opted for prime rib, but Tucker declared he was more adventuresome than they were. He chose the lamb. Without much delay they were all served a salad of mixed greens with a superb herb dressing. Megan took a bite and announced, ''I'm tasting those herbs that I smelled when we first came in, only with a bit of dill added.'' She talked only a little after that, for the rest of their dinner was served very promptly. She found she was hungrier than usual. The highly eventful day and the fact that she was eating later than normal probably accounted for that. She concentrated on the appetizing food before her, saying little, just listening to Tucker and Joe.

"Say Megan, I just realized something. You're the one who made a hero out of Tucker." Joe grabbed her attention just as she was adding another dab of sour cream and chives to her baked potato. It took her an instant to zero in on what he meant.

"Yeah, I guess you could say that. He did a heroic thing, risking his life for me, certainly." She turned her smile to Tucker. "Thank goodness you were there for me that day, Tucker."

"I was destined to be there," he said, giving her a knowing look.

Joe arched one eyebrow wryly. "Oh, come off it, Tuck. You saw a chance to make a lasting impression on a good-looking woman, and you took it."

Joe's teasing banter got them all going along with quips and fun talk. They chatted comfortably together as they enjoyed their meal and lingered over a sinful chocolate dessert and coffee. Finally Joe pointed out that most of the diners had left and probably their waiter would be relieved if they did the same.

It was a pleasant ending to an eventful day, Megan thought as they said good night, then waited for Joe to drive off before Tucker started his car. Outside it was a rather spectacular night. A full moon, white as a china plate, sailed high in the sky, filling the night with a silver light. This made for a ghostly effect, most appropriate for this time of year, with Halloween only a few weeks away.

Fifteen minutes later they were driving into Megan's driveway. ''I know it's been a long day for you,'' Tucker said, switching off the ignition. ''But just stay out here long enough for me to thank you for what you did today.''

''You mean for going up in the air with two daring men in their flying machine?'' she quipped.

''That's only one of the things.''

''You mean there's more?'' Her eyes sparkled with interest. She was able to see his face clearly, as the coach lantern by the front walk was lit, as well as the lamps above the garage doors. Noting his good-natured expression and the tiny smile lines that radiated from the corners of his eyes, she said coyly, ''What other adventuresome thing did I do to merit your gratitude?''

''You were terrific with Evan's aunt. She wasn't comfortable with me. I saw that right off the bat. But you were so understanding and sympathetic with her. I'd have blown the whole deal without you.'' He moved closer and cupped her face in his hands. ''I don't think you realize what a compassionate person you really are.'' Tucker's voice was low and she barely heard it through the pounding of her heart, as his fingers moved along her cheeks and then lifted her chin as he bent down to kiss her. She moaned against the touch of his mouth exploring the softness of her lips. He kissed her deeply, lingeringly, while her senses were spinning. Slowly his arms went around her and he pressed her close. A surge of hot blood rushed to her head and spread like fire through her as the pressure of his embrace increased.

When they finally drew apart, Megan raised her eyes to his and they stared wordlessly at each other. Inside, the car was filled with silence and with the beating of their hearts, which neither of them heard. The silence between them was full of wonder and of promise.

Chapter Twelve

The following day was Sunday. And although Megan was seldom at the hospital on weekends, she was headed there today. A quiet Sunday afternoon meant she could have plenty of time to search the records without interruptions. This was exactly what she intended to do.

Since hospital patient files were stored on microfilm and kept indefinitely, Megan felt confident that whatever took place with Arlene Kane and her infant daughter inside St. Mark's would be recorded on that microfilm. She intended to review every scrap of information she could find. She wasn't going to overlook anything that might possibly aid her in locating Evan's sister.

Tucker had offered to come to the hospital with her if he could be of help. She turned down his offer. "Your being there would only distract me," she told him.

"Well, I certainly hope so," he'd countered with a teasing laugh. "And incidentally, that's one of the most encouraging things you've said to me."

Since Megan wouldn't let him join her at St. Mark's, he insisted that she come to his place when she was through and he'd charcoal steaks on the grill for their dinner. Tucker lived in a hilly, wooded area, and the October winds caused the autumn leaves to fall in a shower of gold, bronze, tan, and scarlet, making a Persian carpet of the ground around his chalet-style house. She smelled the odor of hickory chips from Tucker's outside cooker as she hurried up the brick walk to his front door.

"Sorry I'm late," Megan apologized as Tucker opened the door and led her inside. "I was trying to run down the whereabouts of the resident who took care of Arlene Kane that night in the ER," she explained, following Tucker into his marvelous kitchen and family room with dining el—one large, open, comfortable space in keeping with the idea of living in the kitchen.

"And did you?" Tucker asked, walking over to

the refrigerator and taking out a pottery jug.

"I'm working on it. I've got to check out a possible lead."

"I want to hear about it, and everything else you learned today," he said, filling two glasses with light-amber liquid from the jug. "Let's sit over there and you can drink this and we'll talk."

She eyed him with a leery expression on her face. "I'm suspicious of something that comes out of a brown earthenware container and doesn't have a label. What is that, anyway?"

"Well, it's nothing illegal, if that's what you think." He laughed. "It's pure, fresh, sweet apple cider. A patient of Evan's who has an orchard in Arkansas brought each of us a jug, and he also brought a big round pumpkin. Said I was to carve a jack-o'-lantern and display it in our office for Halloween." He handed her glass to her as soon as she sat down on one of the pair of muted raspberry-colored sofas that stood on either side of the woodburning fire place. "Drink it, it's good for you."

"You mean like 'an apple a day keeps the doctor away'?"

"Stop trying to be cute, Megan. Nothing is going to keep this doctor away from you. Just give it up and drink the darn stuff."

She obediently lifted her glass, suppressing the

teasing laughter that curved her lips and danced in her eyes. "Delicious," she commented as soon as she tasted the cider. "Just what the doctor ordered."

"Touché!" Tucker scowled, feigning disgust at her mocking him. "Now cut it out and tell me what you learned today."

"Not a whole lot that we didn't already know, I'm afraid. But I did learn that the resident who was on duty that night in the ER and delivered Arlene Kane's baby was a Dr. Prayson T. Xanderis."

"That's some handle. There shouldn't be more than one Xanderis in the American Medical Association directory. Did you look him up?" he asked, sitting down on the sofa beside her.

"Yeah. But believe it or not there are two doctors named Xanderis in the United States. Prayson Tyree and a Malcolm Dexter, I think it was. The one we're looking for is listed at the Mayo Clinic in Minnesota."

"Good. We'll put a call in to him first thing tomorrow morning." He leaned back, sipping the liquid from his glass contentedly. "Looks like we may have our first lead."

"I just hope it'll pan out," Megan said with a sigh of frustration. "This doctor is all we've got to go on right now."

''Tell me what you're hoping to learn from this Xanderis.''

''Mostly I want to know about Arlene's baby. Who the doctor was who took care of her after she was born. Maybe find out what nurse was in charge of the intensive care nursery unit. What actually happened to her. Did she die? We don't even know that.'' Megan shrugged, a frown of impatience marking her brows.

''What did it say in her file? Surely some of this information was in that.''

Megan's frown darkened. ''There is no file, Tucker. That's just it!'' Her voice rose sharply.

He shook his head in disbelief. ''That's impossible. There has to be a hospital record on that baby.''

''Well, believe me, there is not!'' She spoke emphatically. ''That's what took me so long. I looked for her under every possible spelling of Kane. Cain . . . Cayne . . . Cane . . . Kain . . . Kayne—I even tried it with two n's, Kanne and Canne. Believe me, I tried every combination of letters that could remotely resemble the right name. There was nothing. The only mention of that baby is in Arlene's file, which merely states that the patient, Arlene Kane, died during the delivery by C-section of a female infant. It's like she disappeared after she was born.''

"Well, we know that she was here. Dorcas and Jim saw her in the incubator, hooked up to all that medical equipment. A doctor talked to them about her respiratory condition. Somewhere in this hospital there has to be a record of the treatment she received, how long she remained in this hospital, and what agency or person assumed care of her when she was discharged from St. Mark's. Those answers are in those microfilm records someplace. They're required to be." He nodded with a taut jerk of his head.

"I know they are," she agreed. "But you can't find them under the name of Kane. That I'm positive of."

"Weird, isn't it?" Tucker said, a grim smile stretching across his lips.

"You can say that again. This day was a total bummer. I didn't really find much of anything for us to go on." Her dejected tone echoed the disappointment that marked her face.

"Hey." He pulled her into the crook of his arm. "You done good, kid. You found this P. T. Xanderis guy. I'll bet you he can shed some light on this when we talk to him Monday. In the meantime," he said, kissing the tip of ear, "we're going to stop brooding, because I'm thinking of much more fun things for us to be doing right now." He kept his lips close to her ear and his words were a come-hither growl.

His teasing brightened her mood considerably. "Yeah, me, too," she countered with a bright laugh. "Like cooking our steaks and eating dinner."

"That isn't exactly the number-one thing on my agenda," he grumbled, continuing to nuzzle her ear.

"It is on mine," she piped gaily, jumping to her feet and holding her hand out to Tucker. "Let's go—I'm starving."

First thing Monday morning Tucker hired an investigator and Megan put in a call to Prayson Xanderis in Rochester, Minnesota. Shortly before noon Dr. Xanderis returned her call. She quickly explained her connection with St. Mark's Hospital and then as briefly as she could explained the reason for her call. "I know all this happened twenty-six years ago, but I'm hoping you can recall the circumstances of that night and what happened to Arlene Kane's baby."

He didn't answer right away. Megan held her breath, fearing he was going to tell her that he didn't recall anything about the incident.

"I was just a second-year resident at that time,"

he said finally. "And yes, I do remember it very well. Probably because while I'd assisted with several C-section deliveries, I'd never performed the entire procedure on my own. To be honest with you, I'm sure the reason I still remember it now is because I was a little nervous about doing it. Had a bona fide case of stage fright—or delivery room fright, I guess you'd call it." He gave a self-deprecating laugh.

"That's certainly understandable. I can't imagine any more extreme circumstances than the ones you had to face."

"It was a traumatic case, that's for sure. That woman had been seriously hurt in that tornado and she was barely alive when they brought her into the emergency room that night. Too, her condition put her baby in jeopardy. I knew I could lose both of them if I didn't move fast." He paused and Megan somehow sensed that he'd been about to add something and then thought better of it. "That's about all I remember, and I'm afraid I haven't been of much help as far as what happened to the child."

"But she did live."

"Oh yes."

"Well, it's certainly strange that there's no record of her receiving nursery care at St. Mark's."

"Hmm, that *is* odd. I can't understand how that could be."

"Would you have any idea what doctor might have been put in charge of a premature baby who was in such critical condition as the Kane baby?" she asked, prodding him for some answer, any answer, that might give her a lead to pursue.

"I don't know, but I'll tell you who would know that if he's still around, and that's Bruce Samuels. I trained under him and, as a matter of fact, he was in the hospital that night delivering a baby. He heard I was in the middle of an emergency cesarean, so as soon as he finished with his delivery he came in to help me out."

"Oh, I've known Dr. Samuels all my life. And he's very much around. St. Mark's wouldn't be the same without him. He and my father were great friends. You may have known my dad, Dr. Manford."

"Oh, my gosh! Of course I knew Adam Manford. When you told me your name I just didn't think to make the connection," he said in such a genial tone that Megan knew he had to be smiling. "Well, you've got your answer right there," he continued. "Obviously your father would have been the pediatrician best qualified to care for an infant in such critical condition as the Kane baby.

You check that out and I'll bet you'll come up with some answers you need. Good luck to you," he told her as their conversation ended.

As soon as she hung up from talking to Dr. Xanderis, she dialed Tucker's office. He was with a patient, so she told his nurse she'd call later after she got back from lunch. She headed immediately for the hospital cafeteria and got a tuna salad sandwich and some pears and cottage cheese that looked appetizing without having an exorbitant number of calories.

As she looked around for a place to sit, she spotted Emmy Walker eating alone at a table. Emmy was one of the oncology nurses in the cancer treatment center. Megan had met and talked to her a few times when she and Tucker had been there to pick up Evan following his chemotherapy.

"May I join you?" Megan asked when she came up to her table.

"Sure you can," Emmy said, her dove-gray eyes crinkling as she smiled. "I was hoping I'd see a familiar face around. I don't relish eating by myself. I have to do it too much of the time, and frankly it's boring." She made a grimace like a squeezed orange.

"I feel the same way," Megan agreed. "Food even tastes better when you've got someone to talk with while you eat."

The friendly nurse studied Megan's face for a moment. "Oh, now I've placed you," she exclaimed, bobbing her head and pursing her lips in a satisfied expression. "You're one of Dr. Kane's friends and we've talked a time or two when you've come to pick him up at the cancer center."

Megan nodded. "That's right. I've come in with Dr. Hadley a number of times. He and Dr. Kane are in practice together."

"Yes, I know who Dr. Hadley is. But I don't think he's come for Dr. Kane any this last week. It's been a pretty blond, and she's come by herself."

"Oh, that's Linda. She's Evan's girlfriend."

"I gathered as much," Emmy said with a knowing smile. "You should see how he brightens up when he finds her there waiting for him."

"I can imagine," Megan said. "Linda's doing little caring things for him would mean everything to Evan. He needs this so much right now." There was poignancy in Megan's words. Then realizing she'd said more perhaps than she should have about Evan, Megan quickly steered the conversation into a light impersonal vein while she ate her lunch. She and Emmy chatted easily and pleasantly together for another twenty minutes before they headed back to their respective jobs.

*   *   *

Several people were in and out of Megan's office during the afternoon, so it was late in the day before she thought again of her conversation with Dr. Xanderis and his mention of Bruce Samuels. Now she reached quickly for the phone to check and see if Samuels might happen to be in the hospital.

"Sorry, but Dr. Edwards is taking over for him. Do you want me to put Edwards on page?"

"No, it's not a medical problem," Megan said, "but thanks anyway."

She then tried calling Dr. Samuels's office. When she got his answering service, she was told that he had gone out of town to his nephew's wedding and wouldn't be back in his office until the end of the week. *Rats! What a bit of rotten luck,* she thought, heaving an exasperated sigh. "I'm stymied," she muttered.

"Who's stymied?" Tucker asked, walking in the door.

"Oh, I am," she complained, wrinkling her nose like a distraught rabbit. "Just when I think I'm about to get some helpful information, I get put on hold. It's frustrating."

"Enlighten me. Is it about Evan?" He had come over to her and now stood in front of her desk looking down at her. His eyes were filled with a strong intelligence that was now quietly and alertly waiting, studying her.

She still had one hand resting on top of the phone. She shoved the phone aside and propped her elbows on her desk and rested her chin on the back of her hands. "It's about a lead I got from Dr. Xanderis when I talked to him this morning. He said that Bruce Samuels was in the hospital at the time he was delivering Arlene Kane's baby. He even said Samuels came in the delivery room to see if he could help. Xanderis was a second-year resident at St. Mark's at the time. He'd worked under Samuels in his obstetric training."

"Great! Sounds like you hit pay dirt with this Xanderis fellow."

"Well, to some extent. He knew what went on in the delivery room, but he couldn't tell me what happened with the baby after that. He said Samuels would be the one who could tell us about that. And that's where I'm stymied." She joined her palms together, laying the two index fingers against her lips in a traditional mime's gesture indicating perplexity, and gave a brief shrug and despairing laugh. "You see, Dr. Samuels is out of town at some family wedding. He won't be back until the end of this week."

"Then we'll simply have to wait patiently for his return," Tucker said stoically.

"Patience isn't one of my virtues, Tucker. And I don't think it's one of yours, either. Certainly not where Evan is concerned."

"I know. But like you say, we're stymied for a few days and we're going to have to make the best of it." He shoved his hands in his pockets, lifting his shoulders in a resigned sort of way. "Think of it this way. Three days ago we didn't know Evan's sister existed. And in just two days you've located and talked to the physician who delivered her. Even gotten a firsthand account of what took place here in the hospital that fateful night. I'd say that we've both learned quite a bit in about forty-eight hours." His expressive face was serious, his voice calm. "In another three to four days Samuels will be back, and with luck he'll provide lots of the answers we need."

"You're right, of course. I'll simmer down and while I wait to talk to him I'll see if I can locate a nurse who took care of the newborn babies around that time. Too, Dr. Xanderis felt that my dad more than likely would have been put in charge of a preemie in as critical condition as the Kane baby. If Dad took care of her, there has to be detailed records. He'd have seen to that." She stated this emphatically. "And I'm determined to find those records in these next few days before Dr. Samuels gets back." She squared her shoulders, thrusting her chin up at a confident angle.

Tucker sat down on the corner of the desk looking at her, a detached smile about his lips. "Speaking of seeking out records, I got my first report from Castleton late this afternoon. In fact, that's what I came over to the hospital to tell you."

She gave him a questioning look. "What's Castleton?"

He cocked his head at her. "Not a what, but a who," he said, a wry but indulgent glint in his eyes. "He's Greg Castleton, the investigator I hired to help us locate Evan's sister. He flew over to the state capital this morning to get copies of Arlene's death certificate and the baby's birth certificate."

"Did he get 'em?"

"Yeah. He also checked to make sure there was no death certificate on the baby. Fortunately there wasn't. At least that proves definitely that she did not die here in the hospital, and if she was either adopted or raised in a foster home here in the state that would indicate that she's still alive and maybe even living in this area."

"But who raised her? We have to learn that first. Why, right now we don't even know her name." Megan's voice was filled with despair.

"Castleton's already working on that. He told me he had a good contact in Social Services. He thinks we can learn fairly quickly whether she was put in a foster care program or not. If she was adopted, then we may need some legal help. Usually adoption records are sealed, you know.''

Megan nodded. ''I've heard that, and they always play up such obstacles in the daytime soaps on TV.''

''You're my partner, Megan, and together we're going to overcome the obstacles, whatever they turn out to be,'' Tucker said with conviction. He had an expression, a tightening of the lips and a lowering of the eyelids, that was unfamiliar.

His words seeped into her mind and for several beats of her heart she looked at him. *''You are my partner, Megan,''* he'd said. ''Partner'' had several depths of meaning. She wondered how much, or how little, Tucker meant by it.

Chapter Thirteen

Megan could smell the sharp scent of the pine trees and hear the gentle wind moving with autumnal sadness through the branches as she walked from the hospital to the service station where she'd left her car that morning. It had been time for an oil change and she'd also bought two new tires that needed to be mounted, and then the wheels balanced. The Texaco station only six blocks from the hospital offered full service and had an excellent mechanic whom Megan relied on for everything her four-year-old Escort ever needed.

She wasn't in any particular hurry, as she had thirty minutes before she was to meet Tucker at the lawyer's office. She ambled along and watched an occasional yellowing sycamore leaf drift slowly down and land on the sidewalk at her feet.

So far the day had gone well. Since it was Thursday, Megan had called Dr. Samuels's office, hoping to find that he was back in Claysun. This time she was able to talk to his nurse. She assured Megan that the doctor would be returning later that day and that she could reach him after eight tomorrow morning.

It had been only a few minutes after that when Tucker telephoned. "I just got a call from Castleton," he told her. "He's found out that Evan's sister was never in foster care. She was adopted while she was still in intensive care at St. Mark's." Tucker's usual calm voice was edged with excitement. "Now that's the good news; however, the adoption files are sealed and it will take a court order to get them released." He reported all this information in a fast flow of words, and it seemed to Megan that he didn't pause even once to catch his breath.

"How difficult is that? Can we get one—a court order, I mean?" she asked anxiously.

"I think so. We'll need a lawyer, of course. I intend for us to go talk to one today. I was going to try to get an appointment as soon as I spoke to you about it." He paused for a second, then continued in a thoughtful tone of voice. ''I was wondering what you might think of our using the lawyer Linda works for, Maurice Burkwald?''

''Tucker, that's a great idea. It's super of you to have Linda be a part of this. Just think what it will mean to her to feel she helped find the donor for Evan.'' She breathed a gentle sigh before adding, ''It will mean a lot to Evan, too, you know.''

''Yeah, I know,'' Tucker said. ''Because the four of us are in this together—all the way.''

The emotional tremor in Tucker's voice brought tears to Megan's eyes. She could never doubt that he was a kind and caring man. In the past he may have had some reservations about Linda, yet certainly today he'd shown his thoughtful consideration of her feelings. Megan wished they could have had this conversation in person, so that the emotion she'd heard in his voice, she could have seen in his eyes. His sensitivity caused feelings of tenderness that tugged at her heart. If she hadn't known it before, she knew now how special he was to her, and how much she cared about him. He was the man she loved and wanted. Out of the days of her life, Tucker was the one, and only one, she would have loved in childhood as well as in youth, if she had known him. She breathed a pensive sigh, wondering if Tucker had any such feelings about her. Then before she let herself drift into wistful melancholy, she quickened her steps.

When Megan arrived at the law firm of Shelton, Graham and Burkwald, she found that Tucker was already there. He was engaged in serious conversation with Linda in one corner of the well-appointed, rather impressive reception area. From the expression of wonder and intense interest registering on Linda's face, Megan knew Tucker was telling her about Evan's sister and the necessity of finding her for a bone marrow transplant.

Megan barely had time to say hello to Linda, before she and Tucker went into Maurice Burkwald's office. After conferring with him, Tucker appeared highly optimistic. Burkwald said he would need medical statements from Evan's doctors about his cancer, detailing the treatments that he had undergone and his need for a bone marrow transplant. He assured Tucker that the fact that there was a life-and-death question involved should help them obtain a court order for access to the adoption file on Evan's sister without any problem.

''You know what we have to do before the day is over,'' Tucker said as they left the lawyer's office.

"Talk to the cancer center about those medical statements we have to have on Evan." Then with a confident flip of her head, she added, "I'll take care of that the minute I get back to the hospital."

"Good, you do that. But that wasn't what I was thinking of."

Surprised, she gave him a questioning look. "What then?"

He put his arm around her waist and fitted his steps to hers. "We have to go see Evan and tell him about everything." There was a ring of excitement in his voice and his smile was bright as sunshine. "Wouldn't you like to do that?"

Her smile matched his. "Of course I would. But—" She hesitated, her smile fading as she moistened her lips with the tip of her tongue.

"But what?" he prodded her, frowning curiously.

"You're dropping a real emotional bombshell on Evan, Tucker. I just thought it might be better for both of you, and easier, without me for an audience." A slight nervous reflex caused her to shudder.

"Hey, you're no audience. You're a major participant in all of this." He tightened his hold on her waist, hugging her against his side reassuringly. "You and I are the bearers of wonderful, astounding news for Evan. Believe me, the best possible way to tell him is for us to do it together.''

He stopped walking then, and because he had one arm firmly around her waist he forced her to stop, too. Now he put both arms around her, turning her to face him. His blue eyes met her brown ones. ''I want us to be together in everything, Megan. Do you understand that?'' There was an almost imperceptible note of pleading in his face.

Her heart began to hammer and she could feel her pulse beat in her throat as she considered the possible implications of his words. ''You mean while we're helping Evan?''

He gazed directly into her eyes. ''I mean with absolutely everything,'' he said sternly, a sheen of purpose in his eyes.

Megan's eyes were lit from within with a golden glow and she smiled provocatively. ''Maybe you should explain this to me more fully sometime.''

He pressed her to him, his hands locked against her spine. ''I'd love to do just that,'' he agreed.

''Not now, in the middle of Fourth and Main streets,'' she gasped, twisting and arching her back to get free.

Tucker eyed her in amusement. ''Are you suggesting that my behavior is unsuitable for a doctor and a gentleman?'' he asked, a trace of laughter in his voice.

''I'm saying that at four-thirty in the afternoon

on the busiest street in Claysun I'm not going to risk finding out.''

''Coward!'' Tucker said, his laughter now a full-hearted sound.

Megan's sense of humor took over and she laughed too as they walked on down the street side by side, yet now not quite close enough for even their hands to touch.

When Tucker and Megan arrived at Evan's apartment that evening they found him ensconced in his favorite recliner chair, wearing gray sweatpants and a T-shirt, and his feet cushioned in soft deerskin moccasins.

''Man, do you ever look comfortable—lazy, too,'' Tucker added with a teasing chuckle.

''You're right on both scores,'' Evan agreed. ''I'm just celebrating a milestone.''

''Gosh, don't tell us it's your birthday,'' Megan said, walking over to give him a caring touch on his shoulder. ''We didn't bring a present, a cake, or anything.'' She sounded sincerely distressed.

''Relax, Megan. It's not my birthday, and if it was, then you're coming to see me would be present enough,'' he said, smiling up at her. ''What I'm celebrating is the fact that they're giving me a brief hiatus from chemotherapy. Now if I can get back a little energy I may even feel like going back to work at the office. Wouldn't that be cool?''

"That would be massively cool." Megan tried to sound enthusiastic, but looking at him, she wasn't very optimistic about his chances. Over these last weeks his leanness had become thinness. He appeared so fragile and worn that the sight of him brought tears to her eyes.

"Well, speaking of causes for celebration, wait till you hear this," Tucker chimed in. "Megan and I came over tonight to tell you a fantastic story that you're not going to be able to believe."

Evan eyed his friend suspiciously. "I hope I'm ready for this, ol' buddy. Don't you dare freak me out with one of those wild and crazy tales you sometimes come up with."

"I guarantee this will be the best thing I've ever told you. Megan will back me up on that." Tucker shot Megan a knowing look that ended in a conspiratorial wink. "Tell the man, Megan."

A very touching smile curved her lips. "It's true, Evan. This is one story you do want to hear."

"Okay then. Lay it on me," he said, shrugging his shoulders in mock resignation, then resting his head against the back of his chair.

"Well, first I need to give you some background," Tucker started out in a casual, matter-of-fact tone. "The other Saturday when Megan and I visited with your family, your aunt had something more important on her mind for us than just to bring you back the cookies she'd baked for you.''

Evan chuckled. ''I can buy that. My aunt is a doer of good deeds and she never stops with just one.''

''She's also determined to see you get well. She had something real important that she wanted us to tell you.''

''It's about your mother,'' Megan added.

''My mother's dead. My father, too.'' Evan rubbed his hand across his forehead, shielding his eyes from view as he said this.

''I know. Dorcas told us about the tornado.'' Megan hesitated a second before she said, ''You did know your mother was pregnant at that time, didn't you?''

Evan stared at her, a look of both surprise and amusement on his face. ''I was six years old, Megan. I may not have known the word pregnant, but I certainly was told that I was going to have a baby brother or sister at the end of that summer.'' He crossed his arms across his chest, continuing to eye Megan curiously. ''But I sure don't see why Aunt Dorcas would be telling you about that.''

''Because of what took place when they brought your mother to the hospital that night of the tornado—''

''She died. That's what happened,'' he said

tersely, interrupting Megan before she could explain.

"Yes, tragically she did," Tucker said, stepping into the breach. "But in an attempt to save the baby, they performed a cesarean section and delivered a baby girl. *Your sister.*"

Intense astonishment touched Evan's pale face. "Are you positive this is really true?"

Tucker nodded. "It's true, there's no doubt about it. Dorcas and Jim even saw her in the incubator. She was two months premature, weighed only three pounds, and had respiratory problems."

"But why did I never know about her? What happened to her?" He was breathing in shallow, quick gasps, his face drawn in tense lines. "She died, didn't she?"

"No, Evan, she did not die in the hospital. Even though the doctors did tell your aunt that the chances were slim that she could live. But she did, and that's the miraculous part we're here to tell you." Tucker's voice quickened. "We learned just today that she was adopted, and we already have a lawyer working to obtain a court order to open the adoption files so we can locate her." He leaned over, laying his hand on Evan's shoulder. "Do you understand what this can mean, Evan?" Tucker's voice rose excitedly. "She's your sibling. This wonderful little sister of yours can be your donor.

Her bone marrow will be the match you need!'' he exclaimed triumphantly.

A kaleidoscope of emotions patterned and re-patterned Evan's face. For several moments he seemed oblivious to everything except whatever thoughts, memories, and hopes were now filling his mind. Finally a deep sigh parted his colorless lips, then a smile of wonder brought a radiance to his eyes. He looked from Tucker to Megan, and then back again to Tucker. He didn't utter a single word, nor did he need to. The bond of sympathy and understanding that existed between them could not be expressed in words—it could only be felt in the heart.

Chapter Fourteen

The rain began at dawn. All night the clouds had gathered, drifting up unseen in the darkness. Megan awoke to the hiss of the autumn wind and the sound of raindrops splashing down her windows. She regretted that the morning was getting off to a wet, dismal start. However, she didn't allow it to deter her from taking her new fashionable-length, pencil-slim skirt from her closet so she could wear it with the Black Watch tartan vest she'd bought two days ago at the British import shop. She had no intention of allowing the rainy weather to keep her from looking smartly dressed for her luncheon date with Dr. Samuels.

When she'd gotten home from Evan's last night, she'd found a message from this dear, kindly man on her answering machine. ''Understand you've tried to reach me. Let me take you to lunch Friday. Meet me at noon at the Riverside Grill,'' he'd stated in his usual brusque, no-nonsense manner. But he endeared himself, adding, ''I'm looking forward to eating lunch with my favorite redhead, so don't be late, Megan.''

Knowing she would be taking a longer lunch hour than she normally would, she went in early to work. Luckily, too, nothing unexpected came up at the hospital, so she completed her morning tasks promptly on schedule and walked out to the parking lot to her car at a quarter to twelve.

By now the rain had stopped, but drops of water continued to plop down from the wet leaves of the oak and sycamore trees. Also the clouds still lingered, forming a charcoal-colored canopy over Claysun's Silverline River.

Bruce Samuels was waiting for her when she came in the restaurant. ''You're right on time, Megan, and I like that,'' he said, greeting her. ''Being an obstetrician, the women I see are either early or late—they rarely perform on schedule.'' He made his little joke as he took her arm and guided her toward a table that overlooked the river. ''You know you're like your dad that way. Promptness was one of Adam's best traits. I'm glad to see he passed it on to you.''

Megan made a mild grimace. '' 'Passed' is too mild a word. Shoved it on to me or scared me into it is more like it. Growing up, I honestly thought that to be tardy was a criminal offense.''

''You mean it isn't?'' he exclaimed, feigning surprise. He winked at her then, and they both were laughing as the waiter handed each of them a menu.

They stopped talking only long enough to scan the menu and each make their choice of what they wished to eat. As soon as they had ordered, the garrulous Dr. Samuels again started off the conversation. ''Now Megan, do tell me how everything is going in your work at the hospital.''

''Great. I'm really enjoying what I'm doing.''

''Then you are happy that you came back to Claysun to work at St. Mark's?''

''Yes, I truly am.'' Her voice mirrored her contentment. ''I like living in the house where I grew up. It all just feels right somehow, like right here is where I belong.'' For a moment, after she'd said this, a very touching smile marked her expression.

''Then I take it that you find the doctors and the hospital staff friendly and cooperative. Maybe even one or two doctors more friendly than others.

Am I right?'' he asked, a teasing look in his merry eyes.

How cagey he is, she thought. She knew this old friend of her father's was having fun with her and she was determined to give it back to him in kind. ''Well, of course I admire and respect all you good doctors at St. Mark's. Since you're the doctor that delivered me, I've known you by far the longest, and obviously you're my favorite. And that nice Dr. Hadley, who rescued me from danger, and his friend Dr. Kane have been so helpful to me. And speaking of getting help from some doctors that you know, I had occasion a few days ago to talk to a Dr. Prayson Xanderis. Matter of fact, he suggested I talk to you about the information I need.'' Megan poured all this out in a shower of words, and Samuels appeared nonplussed at how adroitly she had turned the focus of their conversation away from her and onto him.

''Slow down a minute,'' he said, holding his hand up to stop her. ''You're changing lanes so fast I can't keep up with you.'' A frown bristled his shaggy gray eyebrows. ''And who's this Dr. Alexander you're talking about?''

''Not Alexander; his name is Xanderis. He was a resident at St. Mark's in the early seventies, I discovered. He trained under you in obstetrics, he told me.''

Samuels shrugged. ''Well, I've seen a good number of residents come and go in my time. Far too many for me to recall all their names, I'm afraid.''

''Even if you don't remember him by name, I hope you'll be able to remember a specific emergency case that you helped him with. When I talked to him the other day he said you'd be more apt to be able to provide the information I need than he was.'' She leaned her arm on the table, inclining her head toward him. ''This is why I was so anxious to get to see and talk to you.''

Their lunch had just been served. Samuels held up a silencing hand once again. ''You're going to have to indulge me, Megan,'' he said good-naturedly. ''This all sounds too complicated for me to handle on an empty stomach. So let me get started on my crab cakes and you can explain what this is all about between bites of that ladies' something or other.''

''It's a ham and mushroom quiche.'' She smiled and tasted it. ''It's delicious, I might add.''

They ate for several minutes in silence. Then Megan took a drink of water, touched her napkin to her lips, and said, ''I'll try to keep this short and to the point. However, I want to explain enough so that it will strike a chord in your memory.''

"Okay, I'll do my best."

"In June of 1971 a tornado struck someplace in southeastern Kansas. A pregnant woman was critically injured and was brought to St. Mark's emergency room where the resident on duty, Dr. Xanderis, delivered her baby. You were in the delivery room at the time the woman died. But the baby lived. Do you recall any part of this?"

There was a sudden grim set to his mouth and he seemed to be scrutinizing her intently for several seconds before he answered. "I have some recollection of this, but I can't imagine why you would have any interest in a tragic incident that occurred that long ago. How did you even learn about it?"

"From a woman in Roswell, New Mexico, who happens to have been the sister of Arlene Kane, the woman who died in the emergency room that night." Megan's voice became more emotional as she continued. "You see, what you or no one else could possibly know is that Arlene Kane was Evan Kane's mother. And that means that the baby that was born that night is Evan's sister. She's his one and only sibling. So she alone has to be the donor for the bone marrow transplant that can save Evan's life."

Total consternation marked Bruce Samuels's angular face. "There's no possible doubt about this, I suppose?"

"None." She shook her head emphatically. "Our problem now is to find her. You see, there are no records in the hospital as to care and treatment of her after she was born. Not under the name of Kane, at any rate. We did obtain a copy of a birth certificate that lists her as merely 'Kane infant—female, born June 19, 1970 at 11:53 P.M.' It's signed by Dr. Prayson Xanderis. That's about all we could find out on our own. So Tucker hired a private investigator," she said, picking up her fork to eat the rest of her quiche.

"And this investigator, has he turned up any useful information?" Samuels asked, a faint tremor in his voice as though some emotion had touched him.

Megan's face brightened. "He sure has. He found out that Evan's sister was never put in any sort of foster care. She was adopted and taken right from the hospital. Now all we have to do is get a court order to have the adoption files released so we can learn the name of the family who adopted her."

"I don't know whether that's very wise or not, getting sealed adoption records opened," he said, his face clouding with uneasiness.

"Of course it's wise. It's also imperative." Her

voice rose defiantly. "You know how desperately Evan needs that marrow transplant. And besides, what could possibly be wrong with bringing a brother and sister together who haven't even known of each other's existence until now?"

"I'm not saying it's wrong. It's just that we're dealing with strong human emotions here." He hesitated, eyeing her with a calculating expression. "What I actually mean is, what if this young woman has no idea of her background? Never been told that she was adopted? You can't just spring all of this on her without preparing her first. It all must be handled delicately, compassionately." His brows drew together in a worried expression.

Megan's mouth dropped open and she stared at him, a stunned expression in her eyes. "You know who adopted her, don't you?"

"Yes, I do." His voice was calm, his gaze steady.

"Then you know her name, and possibly where she lives," she spoke eagerly, prodding him for answers.

"I know how to get in touch with her."

"Then tell me and I'll get Tucker and we'll arrange a meeting with her." Megan's voice rose, mirroring her excitement. "This is so wonderful. Thank goodness I came to you about it. This means we can be in contact with her in the next day or so. It's a kind of miracle.'' She ran her words together, talking faster and faster in her enthusiasm. ''So tell me now. What's her name and where can we find her?''

''Not quite so fast, Megan. I'll tell you, but all in good time.'' He pushed back his chair and stood up. ''The rain is over and it's nice outside, so let's go down along the Riverwalk and I'll tell you the amazing story about this young woman who is about to learn that she's Evan Kane's sister.'' He held out his hand to her. Megan rose from the table, placing her hand in his. As the two of them walked out of the restaurant, Bruce Samuels turned to her and said, ''You know, I wish your father could be here to tell you all of this, because he's the one who cared for her in the hospital. So he knew more about her than the rest of us who were at St. Mark's at that time.'' He smiled at her, tightening his hold on her hand. ''But I'm certain that he'd be happy knowing I'm here to tell you the whole story.'' His smile etched lines down his cheeks and creased up the corners of his benevolent eyes. Megan found it impossible not to be warmed by his charming manner, which at times like this reminded her a good deal of her father.

After Megan left Dr. Samuels her mind was so crowded with a myriad of thoughts that she was

scarcely aware of how she got from the Riverside
Grill to Tucker's office. Sure, she had to get in her
car, start the ignition, and drive there, but she did
it automatically. It wasn't until she walked through
the door of his waiting room that she was fully
conscious of her surroundings.

"I need to speak to Dr. Hadley for just a few
minutes," she told the woman sitting behind a
glass partition.

"Just write your name and the time of your appointment." She indicated a sign-in sheet on the
counter.

"You don't understand. I don't have an appointment. I do have some important information for
Dr. Hadley and if you'll just tell him that Megan
Manford wants to speak to him for only about five
minutes, I'm *very sure* he'll agree to see me." She
underlined her words emphatically, because she
could see that the unsmiling receptionist was taking a dim view of her request.

"I'll tell his nurse," she said tersely. "She'll
inform you if the doctor can see you."

"I'd appreciate you're doing that. Thank you."
Megan turned and walked over to take a nearby
seat. She could feel the pressure building up inside
her. She laced her fingers together and stared at
her nails, fervently hoping that Tucker would be
able to see her right away. She heaved a shaky

sigh and momentarily closed her eyes, willing herself to be patient and calm.

"Miss Manford?" A woman's pleasing voice caused her to look up. "Dr. Hadley wanted me to tell you that he's with a patient, but he'd like you to wait for him in his office." The white-uniformed nurse smiled and beckoned Megan to follow her through a door and along a corridor off of which appeared to be several examining rooms and a small lab. The door into the lab was open, as were two of the examining rooms. Megan presumed there were patients in the two closed rooms. She felt a twinge of guilt for barging in on Tucker in the midst of his office hours. Probably she should have waited until tonight to tell him, but there was no way she could wait. She was too keyed up. She needed to tell him all that she'd learned from Dr. Samuels. She needed to talk about all the ramifications. And she knew that, more than anything or anyone at this particular moment, she simply needed Tucker.

The nurse ushered her into a room at the end of the hall. "I don't think he'll be too long," the older woman reassured Megan. "There're some magazines on the bookshelves if you like sailing or baseball. Perhaps you know that the doctor and his associate, Dr. Kane, have a sailboat." Her metal-rimmed glasses framed her smiling eyes, but did not disguise the levity in her knowing look.

Megan nodded, smiling back at her. ''Yes, I've been sailing on the *ET* with the two of them. It's a great boat.''

Tucker's nurse didn't seem at all surprised to hear this, but she made no further comments, just turned away and hurried off.

Megan was standing with her back toward the door, gazing out the window. Tucker's and Evan's offices were on the seventh floor of the medical building situated on a slight hill across the wide boulevard from the hospital. From his window she had an ideal view of the entrance to St. Mark's. She was so deeply absorbed in her own thoughts that she didn't realize he had entered the room until he spoke her name and came immediately to stand behind her.

''I came as quickly as I could,'' he said, placing his hands on her shoulders and gently turning her around to face him. ''Something is wrong, isn't it?''

She shook her head. ''No—not wrong. Just strange—and really very important. You see, I've just come from talking to Bruce Samuels. He remembers everything about that night of the tornado. You know, he was in the delivery room when Evan's sister was born.'' She paused, sucking in her breath nervously before she went on.

"More than that, he knows every amazing thing that happened to that little premature baby from then on. He knows the couple who adopted her, he knows her name, and he knows where she is."

Tucker looked at her in amazement. "That's incredible!"

"Yeah, it was totally incredible to me. The answer to everything we wanted for Evan was right here all the time, yet none of us had any way to know it," she said, her voice low and barely audible.

"You mean she's here in Claysun?"

Megan's eyes brimmed with tears. "I mean she's right here, Tucker. I found out today that *I* am Evan's sister."

Chapter Fifteen

It was good that her meeting with Dr. Samuels had come at the end of the workweek. Megan welcomed having a quiet weekend to again replay in her mind all the remarkably touching things her father's friend and colleague had revealed to her. Weekends were the time she could move through her house to her own rhythms, and allow thoughts and memories to flow freely as she accomplished chores that required neither thought nor memory.

This Saturday it was a poignant experience for her to move through this house where she had grown up, this home where she had been brought to live when she stopped being simply "female infant Kane" and took on a completely new identity as Megan Marie Manford. Not only had she gained a new set of parents, but she had also been given a new birth certificate and a new birthdate. She understood about her birth certificate being issued in her name, Megan Marie Manford, with her adoptive parents listed as her birth parents, because that was done in adoption cases. But altering the time and date of her birth seemed odd to her, even though Dr. Samuels had given her a plausible explanation. He said that Arlene Kane had died at eleven fifty-three the night of June 19, 1970, and Dr. Xanderis therefore stated that as the time of birth of the Kane baby. "However, as you now know, I was right there in the delivery room," Bruce Samuels told Megan. "When the Kane woman started into cardiac arrest, I took over for Xanderis and finished the delivery while he worked to try to stabilize the mother. By the time I finished the C-section and we had the baby resuscitated and breathing on a respirator, I looked at the clock and it was 12:05 A.M. and the start of another day. That is the reason that, when Adam and Marie Manford adopted you and I signed your birth certificate as the attending physician, I accurately and confidently stated your date of birth as June twentieth." He had said this in a solemn voice, and with such assurance that Megan would never think of questioning his right to do it.

For the remainder of the morning, Megan found pleasure in walking through the rooms of her house—rooms which responded to her as flowers did, silently but generously, almost giving off perfume. When she went outside, the flagstone patio glistened with moisture from the morning mist and fog, and it was as if she were living in a rainbow, for everything was shimmering and iridescent. Everything was right.

Her mood seemed suddenly buoyant. She spun around and dashed back in the house, grabbed up the phone, and called Tucker. "There's something I want you to do with me tonight," she said the second he answered. "Can you?"

"My, my! That sounds like it has exciting possibilities. Your house or mine?" he asked with a wicked little chuckle.

"Mine, you silly. But don't get any wrong ideas. I just want to make lasagna and have Linda and Evan join us for dinner. If Evan is up to it, that is. What do you think of that plan?"

"I think a cozy twosome sounds a bit more exciting to me. However, I'll be a good sport and not point out that four is a crowd, since we're all cousins."

She laughed. "That's quite good of you. I love your team spirit."

"Well, just as long as you love *something* about me."

"You have many admirable qualities that I love, believe me," she said in a soft, endearing tone of voice. Then before he could come back with a teasing quip, she said, "There's one more thing I'd like you to do. I want you to tell Evan beforehand that we've found his sister."

"Oh—are you sure you want me to do that? I figured you might want to tell him yourself."

"I don't think so." She paused and didn't speak again for a long moment. "Somehow I believe it would be easier for him and me too if *you* told him the whole story. Maybe just say I was already his friend, and now I've learned I'm also his sister. And that I think that has to be the greatest thing that could happen for both of us." Her soft voice had a wistful sound.

"I'll tell him in those exact words," Tucker assured her.

"I'd appreciate it, Tucker, and I'll see all of you here for dinner at seven," she said quickly, then hung up before either of them could say good-bye.

The last week in October brought to full tide the change of color in the autumn leaves. All around Claysun you could pick out the bright scarlet, the salmon pink, and the delicate yellow of the maple clumps, the purple of the ash, the yellow torches of poplars flaming in the breeze along the hills, the gold of beech and birch down along the river, and the wine red of the young oaks along the parkways. It was the warning of winter on the way. But it was also the old Indian promise that before cold there would come a brief spell of Indian summer, one last glow of warmth before the winter frosts.

It was at this time that Evan was to have his bone marrow transplant. Megan went into the hospital the first of that week for a complete workup to ensure donor suitability. The following day, under a general anesthetic, her marrow was aspirated. It was a relatively easy procedure, but afterward she was required to wear a large pressure dressing that had to remain intact for several hours, so Tucker insisted that she remain in the hospital overnight.

She was sitting up in bed, spooning the last smidgen of chocolate ice cream from a very small carton, the ice cream being the most appealing item on her dinner tray, when Tucker came into her room carrying a large florist's vase filled with a dozen or more American Beauty roses.

"Oh Tucker, you've brought me roses—and they're so gorgeous. Thank you." Her voice spiraled, she was so pleased at his thoughtfulness.

"Whoa there." He shook his head. "I can't take credit for these. Better read the card." He set the vase down on the table next to her bed so it was within easy reach.

"My goodness, I can't imagine who'd be sending me flowers. No one knows I'm in the hospital but you. Besides, I'm not really sick or anything."

"All I know is that one of those volunteer ladies was pushing a cart with some potted plants and these roses down the hall, and when she saw me start toward your room she said if I was going into room 1119 would I mind taking these in to you. She was sort of flustered. Said the girl who was supposed to deliver flowers this afternoon had to leave early and hadn't finished up."

Megan listened to Tucker and at the same time extracted the florist envelope from among the roses. She took out the card and read the three words written on it. *Thank you, Sis!* She was so touched by those words that her eyes brimmed with tears. "They're from Evan," she said, as two crystal tears made trails down her cheeks.

Tucker sat down on the side of her bed, and leaning over he gently brushed her tears away with his fingertips. "I'm sure he didn't send you roses to make you cry."

A wistful smile played softly across her lips. "I

know. I'm just so touched by his thoughtfulness, and this whole wonderful business of having a big brother.''

Tucker was looking at her closely, his gaze as soft and caring as the caress of his fingers touching her cheeks. ''I didn't bring you flowers, but I do have something for you.''

''You do?'' A ripple of pleasure tingled through her. ''Can I see it?'' She didn't hide the delight she felt in discovering that he had brought her a surprise gift.

Tucker held up his hand. ''In a minute. You have to hear me out first. There's something I want to tell you before I give it to you.''

Oh—that sounds serious.'' Her face sobered. ''You're not going to tell me that I can't leave the hospital tomorrow, are you?'' she asked anxiously.

Tucker shook his head. ''Don't worry. You're going home tomorrow, I promise you.''

''Good!'' She gave a sigh of relief. ''Actually, Tucker, this bone marrow thing was only a slightly bigger deal for me than giving blood at the Red Cross. And they gave me a glass of tomato juice and let me go home right away.'' She made a sour face at him. ''I bet any other doctor would have allowed me to leave the hospital even this after-noon.''

"Well, I'm not any other doctor. I'm *your* doctor, and you are stuck with me whether you like it or not."

"I like it a lot," she said with a quick smile. "And I know you're taking the best possible care of me."

"That's right. That's my destiny—to protect and care for you. I told you about that once. Don't you remember?" His gaze made a slow search of her face, a glimmer of longing in his eyes.

Megan pursed her lips thoughtfully. "Let me see. It was some old Indian belief, I think you told me." There was now a teasing glint in her eyes. "And because you saved me from harm that first day, your fate was sealed. For thereafter you were destined to keep me safe and sound." She put her hand up to his face, touching with light fingers the three parallel lines in his forehead, the faint crinkle at the corners of his eyes. "Wasn't it something chivalrous like that?"

"Yeah, that was about it." He smiled and then caught her fingertips and kissed them. "That's actually what I was going to talk to you about." There was a tremor of emotion now in his voice, and he took her left hand and rested his cheek against it. "Since I want to be responsible for you forever, I brought you a gift that will last that long." He still held her left hand in his, but he had stuck his right hand down into the pocket of his white physician's jacket. Now he pulled his hand from his pocket, and as he placed a beautiful diamond solitaire on Megan's finger, he added, ''Because, you see, like my love, this ring is a forever thing.''

Tucker gazed down at her now with a look she'd envisioned a hundred times in her fantasies. Then he took her in his arms and held her there as they kissed and held tightly to each other. His warm mouth moved on hers, ardent with passion, igniting a glorious response from her. Her heart wanted to cry for joy, for she could no longer question the depth of his emotion. It was there in his voice, in his touch, in the fierce pounding of his heart against hers.

When he finally took his lips from hers, she sighed and asked, ''Would you mind repeating what you said before?''

He smiled, keeping her close in his arms. ''I said, if you'll let me, I'll love you forever—because I'm a forever kind of guy!''

Megan looked at Tucker, her face radiant and her love for him mirrored in her eyes. ''Believe me, darling,'' she said softly, ''I wouldn't have it any other way!''